COLORED
SUMMER

COLORED SUMMER

MICHELLE McGRIFF

URBAN BOOKS

www.urbanbooks.net

This is a work of fiction. Any references or similarities to actual events, real people, living or dead, or to real locales are intended to give the novel a sense of reality. Any similarity in other names, characters, places, and incidents is entirely coincidental.

URBAN SOUL is published by

Urban Books
10 Brennan Place
Deer Park, NY 11729

Copyright © 2007 by Michelle McGriff

ISBN-13: 978-1-59983-011-7
ISBN-10: 1-59983-011-6

First Printing: May 2007

10 9 8 7 6 5 4 3 2

Printed in the United States of America

Prologue

(2006)

The dinner table was quiet as Thea twisted a blond lock of hair between her finger and thumb and looked over her parents closely—focusing on her father's broad nose and her mother's thick, curly hair. She wondered which one had done it to her. Which one had hid the facts about their life?

Her visit with Dr. Michilan had set her on edge the rest of her day—had her quite paranoid. She hadn't even called Craig to go over the last-minute wedding plans.

"You're quiet tonight," Thea's father began, letting his Texan drawl slip from his lips. Thea loved it when he did that. It made him appear even more handsome than he already was, with his smooth milky face and dark, wavy hair, up against those green eyes, which he'd inherited from his mother. Thea only wondered how much of his face belonged to his late father—the former California senator. Thea had seen only photos of her grandfather, Senator Theo Fairbanks. She didn't remember much about him. From the photos, she couldn't tell much. "Somethin' on your mind?" her father asked, pouring himself more tea, noticing Thea's interest in him tonight. Thea's glance went to her mother now, who was tall and thin, with pale skin, blue eyes, and blond curls. There was nothing racial looking about her . . . she was sort of a Barbra Streisand look-alike.

Where would I start? Thea asked herself. Which one of her parents would she put on the spot?

"Dad, Dr. Michilan gave me some really crazy news today." Thea chuckled nervously, deciding it would be her father.

"What's that?" he asked, his smile tightening. Thea noticed her mother's hands suddenly shaking just a little.

Maybe they did know something after all, Thea immediately thought.

"Mom, Dad . . . ," Thea began after a dramatic pause. However, before she could speak, her mother, Tina, burst into tears.

"Oh my God, what a scandal! A baby before the wedding," she exclaimed, knocking over her tea glass. Thea gasped, scrambling now to clean up the mess. Thea's father stood.

"You're pregnant? Get Craig over here right now!" he demanded.

Thea sat staring at her nearly hysterical parents, before bursting into laughter.

"You two are the most insane people I've ever met." Thea giggled, dabbing up the spilled tea with her cloth napkin. "I know how not to get pregnant." She sighed. "Besides, I'm really quite grown, and, well . . . it's just not that serious."

Her mother cleared her throat and smoothed back her wild mop, blue eyes still crazed looking. "We've tried not to get into your and Craig's business, but I would hope that. . . ." Her mother finally just fanned her hand, not wanting to say the rest of her sentence—not wanting to address Thea's sexuality.

"It's something that came up in my blood test," Thea continued. "You know I went for the prenuptial thing . . . birth control and all that." She cleared her throat, hoping not to cross that line between informing her parents and embarrassing them. "Anyway, something funny showed up."

Her father sat down, concern showing. "This sounds serious."

Thea looked at her mother, who was still breathing heavily, alarmed and shaken at the thought of being a grandmother at only forty-one.

"Mom, sit down, will ya?" Thea requested. Tina remained standing, looking at her husband now for support. "Have either of you heard of the sickle cell trait?" she asked, directing the question to her father.

Tina began wringing her hands; then, as if to control her nervousness, she picked up the empty dinner dishes and headed for the kitchen. Cleaning was Tina's pastime. It got her mind off things—like reality.

"Sure, it's a colored disease," her father said, using the archaic term for blacks and then smiling almost slyly.

"Colored?" Thea laughed aloud. "You are so funny. But, no, apparently, it's not, because I've got it."

Tina burst back into the dining room. Thea rolled her eyes, only to have them meet her father's on the downswing. He shook his head barely noticeably, urging Thea's disrespect toward her mother to end before starting.

Tina was an emotional woman, often overwrought: menopause had become a challenge for both her and the family. Prozac had been good for her. Everyone in the Fairbanks household was happy that her doctor had prescribed it for her.

"I'm not dying or anything. It's just one of those odd flukes that makes me wonder. I mean, it's inherited, and I can pass it on to my kids . . . and"—Thea paused—"and the fact that it's a predominately African American abnormality, at least that's the drift I got from the doc, makes it all the stranger that I have it." Thea spoke almost in a whisper, hoping her mother wasn't listening too hard.

"That's crazy, Thea," Scott Fairbanks, Thea's father, said bluntly.

"And I keloid, too," Thea added, sticking out her leg, showing her father the scar.

"That?" He chuckled. "Give me a break." He sighed, opening his shirt, exposing a large, ugly scar of his own. Thea had never noticed it before. But then again, her father wasn't one to have his shirt off much. He sunburned easily, and so he didn't lie out or swim much in their pool.

"But, Dad, that's a keloid," Thea explained. Scott ran his hand across the bumpy area of his otherwise hairless chest.

As a white man, Scott had often wondered about little things like this—his keloids, the grade of his hair, the way his skin would blotch up in the summertime. No one ever seemed to notice these little things, except him.

Scott thought now about his father, the senator Theo Fairbanks. How he wished he could have talked to him more—shared more of his feelings about things.

"Don't be such a whiner, son," his father would say every time Scott had a problem. "You spend way too much time with your mother," he would add just before disappearing into the study, without realizing that it was his disappearing act that had caused Scott to spend so much extra time with his mother.

Theo Fairbanks had always been working or gone, and now he was dead. It wasn't that they had had a bad relationship; they just hadn't had much of any relationship. Scott often tried to miss him, but there just wasn't much there to miss. However, his mother—that was a different story. Though he fought it, she was truly his favorite girl. Somewhere along the line, she had become his best friend, and he dreaded the shortening of her days.

Emma Fairbanks was a proud woman, though her stature was not quite a match for her attitude. She was petite, and her features were soft and quiet. It was in her eyes, however, that Scott could see the fire, a story left untold.

Remembering growing up, he had only foggy memories, disjointed by time and convoluted. Often he would ask his mother about certain things and people they had encountered in his childhood, only to have her tell him that it all was part of his vivid imagination, that perhaps that's why he was such a good writer now—his imagination.

Scott was a good writer. He had earned a living as a good writer for years, but the "beyond good" story he wanted to write was about his mother. One day he would, though she had assured him her life would be *boring at best*.

He would ask her things, sometimes even trying to trick her into conversation about her life and her past, but she was too quick-witted to fall for that.

"My life didn't really start until I married your father," she would say, letting him know that the next words out of her mouth would be about the *great* Theo Fairbanks.

Apparently, his mother worshiped the man. At least

that was what Scott gathered from the attentiveness that she gave to his memory, as well as to his headstone. Every year, on the senator's birthday, she would drag everyone out to the cemetery to lay flowers on the massive gray slab of granite.

Little did she know that that cool, lifeless piece of stone was very much the way Scott remembered the man.

The following weekend, the Harvest Festival began. Thea and her paternal grandmother, Emma, had started the tradition of attending every year when Thea finished high school a couple years earlier.

As she drove up, Thea could see Emma waiting on the corner as soon as she turned onto the wide street. The houses all looked the same: big. All the lawns were freshly mowed, and the windows sparkled from a fresh washing. Everyone on that street could afford domestic help, and most of them had someone working for them who spoke a language other than English, except for Emma. Sure, she had a window washer; that couldn't be helped. At sixty-eight, she couldn't even think of doing that herself, but as for her lawn and gardening and housework—Emma did all that herself. She drove that mower around her yard as if she were in the Indy 500. After her maid, Josie, died, there had been no replacement for domestic help, either.

In the past, Thea's father used to suggest bringing in someone to help, but Emma balked at the idea so that he seldom brought it up anymore.

"Is this a new car?" Emma asked of Thea's Honda.

"No, Emma," Thea answered, with a slight chuckle. Most of the time, she addressed her grandmother as Emma. "You know I drive this car every day. You getting old on me?" She laughed full on now. "Having a senior moment?"

"You wish." Emma chuckled, looking around at the car, still feeling there was something different about it. But then again, she had been feeling different all day. It was an off day, to say the least.

She had been delaying that doctor's appointment, for she knew what he might say. "*Slow down there, Emma. You're not a kid anymore.*"

"Hogwash," Emma said aloud while looking in the mirror that morning, wondering where the time had gone. Where had that once smooth-skinned beauty gone? While pondering the past, she had felt as if she'd been invaded by a visitor and looked around quickly.

Memories of times, people, and places—long filed away—had come to mind right up front.

Visions of past loves, past sins, past lives.

Memories of her mother had clouded her dreams and floated around her room all of a sudden. Almost like angels.

Her mother believed a lot in angels.

Emerald, the green stone, the precious piece of glass that her mother had seen in a picture book once—that's what she was named for. Emerald Jackson was her name—the girl with the green eyes and the lily-white skin.

The Harvest Festival was more crowded this summer than last. Emma hated crowds, but there was no way she would let on to her granddaughter how uncomfortable she was. She had been in many a big crowd, and something bad would always happen.

"Too many trains of thought all going in different

directions," she reasoned. "Surely, a couple of them are bound to collide," she added.

"Oh, Emma, you are so . . . so . . . profound," Thea teased, giving her a squeeze around her tiny shoulders. Thea wasn't must taller than her grandmother, but being fuller and younger just made her feel so much bigger.

They milled around the tables, looking at the crafted goods for over an hour. Thea felt her stomach growl for the second time. She fought off the sensation, urging herself to hang on a little longer. She had bought her wedding dress a size smaller than what she wore now, and with only two months to go, she was running out of time on this diet plan, which was failing miserably. She glanced over at Emma, who was looking over the tables. She looked tired today. Maybe she hadn't slept well. Maybe she had taken one too many spins on that lawn mower of hers. Maybe today wouldn't be a good day to bring up the *blood thing*, Thea thought.

"Grandma," Thea began, using the seldom-used title. Emma turned to her.

"What is it, pumpkin?" Emma answered her, also using a little-used term of endearment.

"Have you ever heard of sickle cell?" she asked.

Sickle cell, the life-shortening disease that had taken her mother before her time. Yes, Emma knew it well.

"What about it?" Emma said, trying not to allow the question to visibly affect her.

"Do you know anyone with it?" Thea asked her cautiously, clearly noticing Emma's expression growing tight and her words coming out tense. Emma shook her head quickly and walked over to another table. Walking over to the table where Emma was now, Thea sensed her grandmother's dishonesty, though for the life of her, she couldn't imagine why.

The exhibitor was a smooth, dark-skinned young man. Thea read his badge. She hadn't seen that name on a young person before—Noah. It just had an old man's ring to it. He noticed her reading his badge and smiled at her. His smile was bright and inviting; Thea couldn't help but be caught up in his warm face.

"Hello," she finally said, her voice coming out softer than she had planned, almost sounding flirtatious. Why was she suddenly flirting with black guys? She never had before. What was wrong with her today? Thea said hello again, with an effort behind her words this time, making sure that nobody got the wrong impression. He smiled and nodded.

Remembering she had unfinished business to discuss with her grandmother, Thea turned to her, only to find her clutching to her chest a small trinket from the young man's table. Emma's eyes were glazed, and she appeared frozen.

It was like slow motion from that second to the next. Thea reached for Emma at the same time the young man came from behind the table to catch Emma before she hit the ground.

Chapter 1

Emerald

Shreveport, Louisiana, 1952

"Come on in hea, Em'rald," I heard someone call. But, surely, they couldn't be calling me; I hadn't been called that name since I was a child. There was no way I was back home: I'd not left the West Coast recently.

However, looking around, I could see that I was indeed in Shreveport, Louisiana, and I was—yes, I truly was—a girl again. I figured I must have been dreaming. Then again, perhaps my life was flashing before my eyes. I'd heard of such a phenomenon. Either way, I figured you should write this all down; it might come in handy one day,

Normally, I followed my aunt Rebecca's voice only for it to end with a rebuking. "Those Devil eyes," she would say to me . . . for no good reason. "The doorway to a Devil heart, I bet," she would go on. She was a jealous woman. Of course, I could have no way of knowing at that point in my life exactly why Aunt Rebecca harbored so much resentment for me. But it was jealousy. Was my white skin and my straight black hair really enough to draw out so much hatred? Or maybe she was just angry. It was an angry time, and this had been an angry year for colored people. The world around us was changing, and none of us was too sure it was for the better.

Aunt Rebecca's daughter Josie was as black as night, her hair tight and drawn up. I often would hear her screaming echoing through the house. Screams coming as that close-toothed comb was being ripped through the tight nap. Every other Sunday, Josie's ears would be black on the tips from the hot comb's burns.

Somehow, I felt guilty for her pain. I wanted to fix it, save her from it all, but there was no way.

Today I followed my aunt Rebecca's bellow into the small room where my mother lay in bed. I was used to seeing her there, but today was different. Today she looked different. I had a feeling deep in my gut that this time my mother wouldn't be getting up again.

"Emerald." My mother smiled at me while saying all the syllables of my name. She was the only one who did. She then touched my face, letting her thin hand linger there against my cheek as if once again comparing her dark skin tone to my lighter one, or maybe remembering my father's skin next to hers. Who could say? My mother, she was so secretive . . . so deep. I allowed her this moment, though. It never mattered to me how many differences there were between us. She was my mother, and I loved her.

For an uneducated woman, my mother knew more than many scholars I've met along my life's travels since she and I parted. She had common sense, which made her wiser than most people I've known. I could only hope I picked up on some of it.

"Emerald, Doc Waters says I need to be getting my matters in order," my mother said.

Her voice sounded light and airy. All of the normal heaviness that was usually there was gone. It was as if her spirit was already on its way out—as if all the burdens she'd held inside were gone. It was as if she was only hanging on to life by the grace of God, who had granted her just these few more moments with me. My eyes burned with that thought.

"Your matters? Does that mean me?" I asked innocently. She nodded. "Mama, I'm in order," I told her, trying to keep some kind of confidence in my voice, hoping to ease her fears about what would happen to her only child, left alone to fend for herself in this jungle of hatred and prejudice. I also thought that maybe by letting her know she didn't need to waste any time on me, she could use her last few moments to talk about something she enjoyed more.

Aside from seeing death this close up, I knew little else about life and the world around me. I had had to quit school a few months back to help care for my mother. I didn't have many friends. It was mostly members of our church who came around, and they were so filled with preconceived ideas about my life and me that I usually avoided saying too much to them. I had such a desire to learn, to take in everything around me. I knew there had to be more out there than just death and despair. Sometimes the curiosity *ached* in my bones.

"Girl, you ain't in no kinda order." My mother chuckled.

I laid my head on her leg while she stroked my hair. It felt good when she did that.

"Now look here. I know you ain't had much of a life

here seeing after me. You ain't even been able to go through school a few months back the right way, and that's too bad. And with the way things are . . ." She was hinting about my looks, as usual. "Well, I don't expect any of these nice boys around here gone wanna have too much ta do wit cha. . . ." she finished, with a loud humph escaping her curled lips. "Them gossiping heffas at the church done seen about ruining that for ya, calling you all them names," she fussed.

I cringed, remembering all the hateful names I'd been called by my own people. Half-Breed, Cat Eyes, Trick Baby, Witch, and some words too painful to bring to mind. I patted her leg now, calming her down before she started cussing or something even worse. She and I both knew it was all just lies what they said. . . .

"It's okay, Mama. I know I'm not from the Devil," I told her, letting her know that I was fully aware of the names I was called. Of course, I didn't understand a lot of what the words meant, but I knew they were hateful. My mother looked at me for a long time before stroking my long, thick tresses, running my hair through her slender fingers again.

"No, you're not. You are my angel child. And despite how you got here, don't you ever think any less of yourself than that. I've always felt inside that the way you look would be a cursing for you," she said. "Or a blessing . . . It's alls in hows so eva ya uses it," she added. I nodded.

It was true. My white skin and green eyes had left me an outcast within the society in which I was born— a society where both the blacks around me and the whites around us expected me to think, feel, talk, and look a certain way. I didn't fit in, and I really didn't know what to do about it.

"Well, baby. You ain't cursed . . . not altogether," she

began to explain. "But your chances of making it in this place, getting anywhere, are slim to none. But I done made a way for it to be all right for you," she said, sitting up a little in the bed now, pulling her gown tight around her thin body. "You gone haveta leave hea'," she said.

My heart nearly stopped. I could not . . . well, I refused to . . . understand what she was saying. Leave there? And go where?

As she spoke, she got clearer and clearer in her meaning. Despite her love, she, too, had seen me as a punishment for sin—a cursing. Like Aunt Rebecca, she felt that the best thing for me would be to go away—and never be seen again.

"Miss Greta wants you. That white woman has been a good friend to me. She's even seen that I've had my medicines and thangs. And seeing that you got some learning . . . at least it comes easy to ya, she's always wanted you. They're packin' up and moving to St. Louis. And she say . . ." My mother's voice began losing its volume—taken by sickness or possibly sadness and growing regret over the hand she had dealt for me. She cleared her throat as if noticing the loss of conviction in her own words. "And, Emerald, it's best," she said, after explaining the basics of the arrangement she had made with Greta Griffith. A heavy sigh left her hollow chest.

Though I tried to understand her words, the pain stabbed deep. The hurt became nearly unbearable, though I hid it well. I had been sold to the highest bidder, it seemed, and was being shipped out—just like the boys who were leaving to fight a war they didn't even understand. But, to tell the truth, at that moment I would have rather gone to battle in Korea than the jungle I was headed to, in my mind. I was being sent to live among the whites. What could be worse? If I had known that becoming educated was merely a grooming to become a commodity, used and traded like a slave, I'd have stayed ignorant—and happy. My mother had no idea what her words were going to do to me, my heart, and the one person other than herself who I had allowed to enter my world.

My reasoning was bitter, as bitter as the taste that was coming up in my mouth while I tried to form the words, civil words, to change this decision that my mother seemed determined to make. "Mama, everybody is gonna still see that I'm different. Being around white folks won't change me. It won't make me white. They will see the difference." I tried to explain to her, to dispute her talk of this fantasy life she envisioned me having. The one she *just knew* I could have away from Shreveport, living with the Griffiths, living among white people.

"Not white people . . . they won't see nothin'. They don't ever see past beauty—past the skin. You move among 'em, and they won't be able to tell a thang," she said flatly. "They don't look that close. They's *surface* people," she explained plainly.

Every time she explained how I was to leave and why, I was more stunned and amazed at the workings of her mind . . . her thoughts. Who had convinced my mother of this lie? Who had convinced my mother that my life would be better this way? I could not believe a woman as intelligent as she had thought of this craziness on her own.

What had possessed her to make this kind of deal with my life? That I, Emerald Jackson, born of two Negro parents—although one, being of Creole descent, had passed on genes that left me looking like this—should have to give up my race, my background, and become white? Why should I have to do this to survive? Why would I have to pretend to be white? Was that truly what she was telling me to do?

"That's what I'm sayin'," my mother said after I asked her in simple terms if that was her request. "If you gone look like a duck, walk like a duck, quack like a duck, be a duck then," she said in one of the most profound statements I'd ever heard her make. "They're coming to get you this coming Saturday. You're gonna live with them in St. Louis," my mother finally said. I looked for sadness or even regret in her words now but found none. She truly, in her heart, felt she was doing the right thing. How I wished I was older. How I wished I had the dogmatic way of my aunt, where I could just say what was on my mind and in a way that everyone would listen to. I had dreams . . . I had plans, and none of them included what my mother was suggesting to me.

I wanted to learn new things, and maybe I had once or twice even fantasized about leaving Shreveport, but never under these circumstances. I had wanted to go away, like on a trip, the way some of the people in town did. I wanted maybe to go away in glory as part of the civil rights movement I'd been hearing about. So many Negros were rising up . . . getting fired up about being black. I wanted to be just as fired up. But for me, it just didn't seem the same. For me, my leaving had no pride. For me, it was as if I were a sold piece of furniture, and it was a sure guarantee that I would never be back.

Chapter 2

My mother hung her gold locket that my father had given her around my neck when she said good-bye the morning I was to leave.

"This will keep us together. Your father always told me that whoever is wearing it is in the heart of the giver of it," she said, before giving me a light shove, moving me away from her bed. "You're always in my heart, Emerald." She was crying and so was I.

"Come on, gal, don't make this harder than it needs to be," Aunt Rebecca interjected, taking me by my shoulders. I wanted to jerk away, but her grip was tight, as if she'd anticipated it. When she shut the door behind me, I just had to brace up and accept that this would probably be the last time I saw them.

When I left that house on an unseasonably cool summer morning, I never guessed what was at the end of that rainbow for me. But, with a kiss and a prayer, I was about to find out. Dressed in a gingham cotton dress, with bare legs, and a pair of my mother's church shoes, long abandoned after she took to her bed, I was on my way. Bag in hand, I started trudging the five miles down the dirt road to the Griffiths' store. In the part of town where I lived, very few colored people owned cars. I guess, I was not important enough for the Griffiths to come pick me up.

Greta Griffith was a schoolteacher, and her husband, Melvin, ran the local market. He was a big man, with a thick beard and heavy laugh, soft blue eyes, and always, always, very clean hands. Nonetheless, I was filled with apprehension while, reluctantly, I walked toward town.

"Where you off to, wit cho bags . . . ? You runnin' off?" my best friend asked as he joined me on the road. Noah Sampson had been my friend since before I knew right from left. He'd been my confidant and maybe even more.

Noah was blessed. His skin was as dark as a crow. His eyes were large and playful, his smile wide and full of joy, and so were his words. He was always cheerful and positive about life and his future. He would speak about leaving Shreveport and going west, as if it was more than just a dream for him, and I loved to hear him talk about it. Aunt Rebecca said Noah was raised by a fool and, therefore, could only speak the words of one, but I knew Noah meant what he said, and although I never admitted it, I often dreamed of leaving Shreveport with him.

Maybe I even loved him a little bit. Truthfully, I knew I loved him a lot, with all my heart, or at least as much as a young girl of fourteen could love a boy. He was older . . . sixteen, and I can't say he felt the same way about me . . . but I wanted to believe he did.

He'd come from his house, no doubt spying me from afar. I couldn't look at him. A heavy sigh left my mouth instead of words when he jumped in front of me, blocking me from walking any farther. I'm sure a tear slipped out, too, as he, as if suddenly enlightened and without asking anything more, took my bag from my hand and slowly and silently joined me in my journey.

Reaching the fields, we stopped for a while to talk. I knew Noah could tell my legs were not up to this journey, and maybe because of the way my feet turned in, he could tell the shoes were not a comfortable fit as well. I had a while before the Griffiths would miss me, and so I kicked them off and rubbed my aching feet.

"I had a bad feeling it would come to this," he said, handing me a cool pop, bought from the machine we'd passed on our way out of town. I was sure he had spent his last to get it for me, so I freely offered to share it with him. It was a little early in the day to be drinking pop, anyway. He grinned and took a swig before giving it back. Noah didn't go to school; he worked with his father in the fields. It was physical work and far too laborious for a young boy; however, it was the life Noah knew and the reality he lived. Maybe that was why he had such wonderful dreams. I, on the other hand, had gone to school every day and had learned under the watchful eye of Mrs. Griffith until leaving school. Even after, she still always had a lesson for me to do when she visited my mother. Had I known she was secretly grooming me to be her daughter, I would have acted much dumber.

Much of my education I had shared with Noah, teaching him to read and write. Yes, I'd say Noah was more than just my best friend; I had a vested interest in him. "I don't want to go, Noah," I finally said, my words heavy in my mouth, my tongue thick and clumsy. Noah looked around and then put his arm around my shoulder, kissing my cheek quickly.

We sat down low in the cornfield so that no one could see us. It wasn't as if we'd done anything improper, but still, being discreet was always the way with us . . . fear was always the way with us. You never knew when someone would come along and blame you for something you didn't do.

"You gone be fine," he said, sounding wise and older than his years.

"I'm not . . . I'm not," I pleaded, the tears flowing like water now. Noah then kissed my lips to silence me. It was my first kiss and, surely, the most perfect kiss that heaven had ever allowed—salty sweet and full of only the purest of love.

When my eyes opened, they met his, and as if we thought as one, we knew what had to happen next.

I don't really know what we were thinking or how it came into our minds, but within minutes we found ourselves in the living room of Reverend Cotton. He thought we were crazy, demanding to be married this way, as I was just a child, and Noah, a few years still short of being a man. And, besides those facts, we had no consents, no papers, just the heat of love in our eyes. "Being a man of God," Reverend Cotton said, "and with no wishes for the two a ya'll to burn in the fires of hell . . . ya'll's man and wife. Now get on outta here," he barked, sending me and Noah quickly from his house, without so much as a sermon or a prayer.

As if traveling on wings, we were back at Noah's house, surprisingly alone, considering how large his family was. We quickly made our way to the room he shared with his brothers.

"I love you, Emerald," he said to me, this time saying my name the way my mother always did—each syllable, each vowel sounded out meaningfully. "My Emerald eyes," he added before he kissed me again, only deeper this time, with more passion and filled with adult feelings. Noah had older brothers, much older than the two of us, and I figured he knew more about kissing and things like that, having learned about the birds and bees from overheard lessons they were no doubt getting about life.

"I love you, too, Noah," I told him, with promise in my words and without an ounce of fear in my heart.

"I can't let you go without . . . this," he said, sounding shy and a little hesitant as he took off his shirt. "We're married now," he said softly. "We're married like my brother Joseph and his girl, Sable. They're married and so . . . it makes it all right." He paused as if that explanation helped me to understand something.

"I'm glad we're married. I'm never going to leave you. I'm—," I began before he shushed me.

For a moment when Noah smiled at me and said again that we were married now, my heart eased of the pain it had carried. For a moment, I believed I was no longer leaving with the Griffiths. However, Noah knew our marriage was not going to stand up to scrutiny. And, being married wasn't going to stop anything that had been arranged by the powers that controlled our young lives. It was as if he again was dreaming, only this time and for these few hours, he had taken me along for the blissful ride.

I had seen Noah without his shirt many times, but for the first time, I noticed how the years of hard labor had shaped his shoulders and added muscles to his arms. The sight of him quivered my belly and forced my hand to his smooth, hairless chest.

He smiled at me as he lay me back on his bed and climbed up on me. I closed my eyes tight as he spread my knees apart. I nearly screamed as he pushed his way into me, but he covered my mouth just before anything could come out, his face grimacing and twisting in the pleasure he was receiving as he pushed his virginity deeper and deeper into mine. Just then, our eyes met, and suddenly, we both realized the moment that this was in our lives.

All the pain fed by our inexperience vanished now as, with determination, Noah and I worked together to accomplish this act of our love, faster and harder until we were both nearly worn-out. It was just a little longer before Noah, as if becoming one flesh with me, began to burrow his newly established manhood deeper and deeper into my body, deeper inside than I thought possible, until I was sure there was no space between us. It was an ecstasy that couldn't be held in. Finally, we cried out loudly as the tears rolled down our cheeks.

I'd never felt anything like it and was sure I never would again. Noah held me as we together cried pitiable tears.

"I'll find you, Em'rald," he promised while we waited out back at Mr. Griffith's store, on the bench. "And when I get some money, I'ma come after you." We'd finally made it to my destination.

Throwing my arms around his neck, I now made him swear to his words. "Please find me," I whispered in his ear. "I don't want to have to stay white too long." I heard him gulp audibly, as if it suddenly had sunken in what was about to happen to me, going off with the Griffiths to live. It was as if he suddenly realized what I was about to give up. It went beyond our friendship . . . I was about to give up my race. No matter how close he and I had become just an hour before, it couldn't change that fact.

"Hey, you kids . . . knock that off!" Mr. Griffith barked, coming out the back door of his store, catching us in our tight embrace. Jerking from Noah's tight grip, I reached for my locket to give Noah something special, something that would keep us together, but it was gone. Apparently, it had broken during our love-making. All I could hope was that he found it before his brother did. I couldn't have one of them living off the magic of the locket and finding a place in my heart.

"You're my wife, and I love you. I always will," mouthed Noah silently, standing slowly from the bench. I held the tip of his jacket for a long time before he pulled away, obeying Mr. Griffith, who shooed him like a dog.

It was hard to let Noah go that afternoon, and to tell the truth, I could still smell his comforting scent in my nose for a long time after.

I had never worked so hard in my life as I did the day the Griffiths moved their store. After we put the last box on that big moving truck, I thought to myself, *This new life is going to be even harder than the one I had.*

Mrs. Griffith thought it best that I not say good-bye to my mama the day we got on the train, heading toward St. Louis. It was just going to be me and her traveling together on the train, as Mr. Griffith would go with their belongings on the truck. He dropped us off at the train depot, and thus my journey began.

Greta Griffith was a friendly woman, plump and jovial. Her blue eyes danced when she spoke, and she would twist her hair with her thick index finger a lot. I knew that inside her head more went on than what came from her mouth, at least I prayed that to be the case, as outside of teaching me to read and write, she was a little on the dim side when it came to life in general—or at least it seemed.

Someone would ask her how her day was, and she would answer, "Melvin is doing just fine." I noticed that right off; she didn't know how to answer a simple question. Everything out of her mouth was about her husband, Melvin Griffith. He was her world. I never saw what she saw in him, but then again, if you really listened to her speak, it sounded like she actually saw someone else—maybe the man she wanted him to be.

After the train pulled off, Mrs. Griffith turned to me. "So, sweetie, I'm sure you're gonna like living with us. I've found a nice school for you and even a college that I'm sure you can get in to when the time comes. Your mother promised me that you would continue to do well in school."

"Of course, Mrs. Grif—," I started.

"Mother," she corrected quickly. "And you are never to tell anyone that I'm not your mother or that you're colored. Do you hear me?"

"Yes, Mrs. Griffith."

My heart nearly stopped. I know I was staring at her like a crazy coon, because I looked at her until I had actually counted nearly every freckle on her chubby cheeks.

"I'm s'posed to call you Mother?" I asked, with my voice just above a peep.

She wrinkled her nose a little, and then, with pursed lips, while straightening out the tea set that was on the table, she smiled real wide and looked me square in the eyes. "Well. Yes, Emma."

My eyes burned, although I didn't cry. I couldn't cry; I was too sad for that. I felt my mouth open. I tried to say it, but I couldn't.

"My name is Emerald," I did finally manage to mumble.

She acted as though she didn't hear me. "It's hard, I know," she said, now laying her hand on mine.

Just then, the waiter came to our table. He was a tall, handsome black man, with a wide, cheery grin.

He wore white gloves and a sharp, clean uniform and hat. His experience showed, as his words were carefully chosen. He was from the city . . . probably St. Louis. He seemed like the kind of man that would come from there. Hearing my mother speak about my father the way she did, it made me imagine all men from St. Louise were handsome and smooth speaking. So, yes, I believe this man had to come from there, too. He fit the description.

"Will there be anything else, ma'am?" the waiter asked. Greta looked at me. I didn't know what to say, so I just shook my head.

"No. My daughter and I are just fine," Greta said, smiling diplomatically.

The man then looked at me. From his eyes, I could tell he knew the truth. He knew I was no more Greta Griffith's daughter than his. In his eyes, I could see the look of betrayal he was giving me. I turned my head away and looked out the window.

From that moment on, I realized that perhaps my aunt was right and my life was only good for misery. Stroking my neck, I felt the absence of the locket, the emptiness of my aloneness, the breaking of my heart.

The Griffiths' new house was very large. They had moved their business to Milwaukee, Wisconsin, not St. Louis, as they had told my mother. At the time, I didn't question why they had lied to her, because I thought I knew the answer. I really believed my father was supposed to be in St. Louis, and maybe they were afraid he would find me. Maybe Greta Griffith was afraid he would take me from them and make me black again, and there was no chance of anything remotely like that happening in Milwaukee.

Within the month, the Griffiths had opened a little

trading store called simply Griffiths Trading Post, and Mrs. Griffith had become a busy housewife, instead of returning to the classroom. She was very involved with the Presbyterian church. I, being Baptist, wondered how that was supposed to work out for me. I was not one to believe just anything I was told, and what she was telling me from a religious standpoint just didn't hold up to what I believed. However, I went along with her to her functions, with the promise that one day I would get to go to church with my people. I kept waiting for her to let me go. It never happened, and so soon, I just let it go and went along willingly with the Griffiths to their large, lily-white church. I had to believe the Lord was with me no matter where I was. I also had to believe that my mama was looking down on me and smiling, that is, if she was dead. I really didn't know if she was dead or alive, but something inside told me my mother had passed on since I moved with the Griffiths.

Greta Griffith did a lot of praying, and I had to figure it was on account of Mr. Griffith. Despite what I had come to believe about him and his soft, pretty eyes, he was not a very nice man at all, at least not to Greta. Sometimes I would hear them late at night, when the house was dark and quiet. I'd hear them arguing about things. He would curse at poor Greta, calling her out of her name, and then he would say mean things about her as a woman and a wife. Sometimes I would hear him breaking things, and she would start crying. I didn't really understand a lot of what he was saying, but by the sounds of his angry words, I didn't really want to. He was angrier about life than Aunt Rebecca ever could be. I would take her switch over his filthy words any day.

Sometimes Greta wouldn't get up in the mornings,

while Mr. Griffith got ready for work. He and I would be the only ones up in the house, along with the dog.

I loved that dog. Sometimes I found a lot of comfort in that animal. I often allowed it in my room at night. I wasn't used to having a room of my own. I had always shared with my cousin Josie, Aunt Rebecca's baby daughter. She had several daughters, but Josie was the one who was my age, and so we had to share a room together. We fought like cats and dogs as she was jealous of me and spiteful. I knew she was, because no one would be that venomous for no reason, and besides, my mother had told me once that that was just the way it was. But even though Josie and I fought a lot, I missed her.

On the mornings that Greta wouldn't get up, I would make Mr. Griffith's breakfast. He would say I made things better than Greta did. His compliment made me feel funny. I mean, I never thought it was right to be told something like that by another woman's husband, especially when I knew Greta could hear him say it.

"I bet you do a lot of things better than Greta," he would say sometimes, smiling at me while smoothing down his bushy beard with his big hands.

"I don't think so, Mr. Griffith. I really don't," I would answer.

One morning in particular he had started his flattering talk with me, going on and on about my coffee and eggs and whatever else I had made, and I sat before him and decided to at least try to get him to stop. "Mr. Griffith, I think Miss Greta is just as good a housekeeper as anyone. And, as a wife, I think she's about one of the best," I said, building her up.

The night before there had been a doozy of a fight between the two of them, and I knew some of the things he had said to her must have hurt deep, because my own heart was paining for her.

"Yeah, well, I don't know about all that," Mr. Griffith said, looking me over from head to toe. "I bet you'd make a good wife," he said, leering at me. He made me feel like the slices of pork bacon I had fried up in that skillet, staring hard at my legs, licking his lips. I wanted to run out of that kitchen, but I didn't.

"I have a long time before I even have to think about being a wife to anyone, Mr. Griffith," I said, smiling tightly.

"Why don't you call me Daddy?" Mr. Griffith licked his lips suggestively.

My stomach flipped over like an egg, and I felt instantly sick. "I . . . I don't know if I can, Mr. Grif . . ." I stammered.

He then outstretched his hand for me to take it. I didn't know what else to do, so I took his hand. He squeezed my hand tighter than it had ever been squeezed before. It really hurt. I tried to pull away. "Mr. Griffith, you're hurting my hand," I protested, with tears coming to my eyes.

"Call me Daddy," he said again, locking his eyes on mine, demanding it.

"I can't," I whimpered.

Suddenly, he pulled me onto his lap and held me tight to him, stroking my hair. "Call me Daddy, Emmy . . . please," he begged.

My stomach felt queasy, and I thought I would vomit. I had to get away from him, so I began to reason on the easy road. How hard could the word be? *Stop being so stubborn, girl,* I fussed at myself.

"Emma," he said firmly, holding my hair in his hand, pulling my head back so that he could see my face. I could smell the fried foods on his breath.

"Daddy," I finally said, choking on the word. Letting

his hand slide down to my thigh now, I felt the release of his grip and jumped up from his lap. And just in time, too, as Greta appeared in the kitchen, wearing a tatty-looking robe, her hair up in pin curls. She wasn't smiling.

"Emma, get on to school," she barked at me, shortening my name the way she did to people's names sometimes. Little did I know that was to become my name from that point on.

At school that day, I was very disturbed about what had happened that morning. It stayed on my mind most of the day. Even my friend Trudy noticed my disturbance. Her name was Trudy Paxton. I called her Peachy. She thought it was funny that I had nicknamed her, as no one had ever done that before. I couldn't believe no one saw her that way. She looked just like a peach to me. With her rosy cheeks and strawberry blond hair, she looked in bloom all the time.

Peachy found many of my habits interesting. She found my thoughts on life to be interesting, often saying that I reminded her of their colored cleaning woman—always talking about things in such a way that made it impossible to understand without a lot of thinking. Peachy loved my hair and the thickness it had, the natural curl it took upon getting wet. It always took everything in my power not to tell her why Emma Griffith looked like she did. But I was sworn to secrecy, and as far as everyone knew, Greta and Melvin Griffith were my natural-born parents.

Peachy and I often went to the picture show and to the soda fountain on the weekends when the Griffiths allowed me some free time. I was always amazed how no one ever questioned me about being there with the white kids. I sat where I wanted and ordered what I wanted and actually got served in the order I arrived in. It was a strange revelation, considering the growing fervor of the civil rights movement in the South.

I read the paper regularly, even between the lines, and listened to the radio as often as I could. Once I managed to even get a letter written to my mother, although I have to say, I'm not sure if she ever got it. I was desperate to make some kind of connection to my life, a life that was, oddly enough, becoming my secret past. Even Noah seemed to be only a dream to me now, someone I used to know.

"What's got you bugged today?" Peachy asked me, sliding onto the bench, next to me. We were in the school yard at lunchtime. She had a brown paper bag, containing her usual egg salad sandwich.

"What's it to ya? Nuthin' for ya," I snapped. I saw her flinch at my tone, and so I told her I was sorry.

"Gosh, you're wrapped tight," she said, seriousness covering her face.

"Nothin' really. Mr. . . . . my parents . . . they're fighting again," I divulged. I had told Peachy about the Griffiths' fights. She swore she wouldn't tell anyone, and Peachy was one person I knew I could trust.

"What a bad scene," she said, letting out a sigh, sharing my misery. Peachy envisioned herself as a cool cat. She swore one day she'd be on television and secretly had a crush on Ed Sullivan. She watched his show every Sunday. She liked to dance and listened to dance music as often as she could get away with it, considering it was all but illegal in that town.

Just then, Jerry Hastings and Keith Mitchell walked past. Peachy really liked Jerry a lot, and although he liked to pretend he didn't notice her, he did. I knew Keith liked me. He often would stare at me during history class. His eyes were dark and soulful, but I figured there wasn't much behind them, and even if there was, I wasn't even halfway interested in finding out what. He was just a rich white boy who thought the world owed him something, and maybe it did. But I didn't.

As they passed, Peachy, unable to contain herself, gave Jerry a flirty wave. I had told her not to be so forward, but she just couldn't resist. In the meantime, Keith called out my name. I ignored him.

"How do you do that, Em?" Peachy asked me.

"What?" I replied.

"How do you stay so cool around boys?"

"I'm marr—," I began and then quickly corrected myself. I was no nimrod. There were bits of information that even Peachy wouldn't keep to herself. My being Negro was one, and my being married was another. There was no way even Peachy would be able to keep those two juicy tidbits under wraps. "I have a boyfriend," I answered, thinking of Noah, the boy I had left behind in Shreveport. The one and only boy I felt I would probably ever love—my husband.

"You do?"

"Oh yes. His name is Noah," I told her. Suddenly, I noticed her face wrinkle up.

"Noah? What kind of name is that?" she asked.

"What do you mean?"

"Noah . . . What is he? That name sounds like a Jewish name. Like Asharef Bernstein. You know him, right? Their family is Jewish, and that's not good."

"Why?"

"Because they're Jews. Jews in Wisconsin? What are they hiding from? That's what my father asks all the time," she went on.

"Well, your father is a bigot, and . . ."

"Oh my gosh, here we go. And that means?" Peachy sighed, reluctantly giving in to my high interest in political matters and the new information floating around regarding race relations, written by white liberals who strived for equality. I'd always had an interest in matters concerning the freedoms of others, and since living with the Griffiths, I had to admit the freer access to the library had given me a windfall of information at my fingertips. I was to the point of being nearly dangerous. Mrs. Griffith had lied on my papers and said I was sixteen, therefore landing me in my junior year of high school instead of the ninth grade, the grade I should have been in. She felt I was smart enough and wanted me in college as soon as possible.

One good thing about a white high school, the books were bigger, better, and I often ended up with my hands on political propaganda, which was nowhere proper reading material for a girl my age. But reading it was something to do while living with the Griffiths, something other than listening to them fight and playing with their dog. It was something to do with my mind while missing my mother and craving my home and family and Noah. Since his touch that summer afternoon, my body had burned at night . . . a burn that started deep in my belly, creeping downward. I was scared to death to touch myself there, for fear the heat would burn me. Sometimes I would simply get up and run a bath, sitting in the tub of cool water until the feeling passed. It would be only by seeing Mr. Griffith's face in the morning that the feelings would cool off completely. Seeing Mr. Griffith's wanting eyes could cool hell enough to almost trick the unaware into stepping on over into it, but not me.

"Essentially, a bigot has no legitimate cause for hostility toward Jews or any racial group of people," I told Peachy. "They have an irrational generalization and negative exaggeration or perception of an ethnic group's physical or moral traits, which is either utterly groundless or . . ." I began reciting the words I'd read and memorized. Peachy tossed her strawberry blond mane and gave me a look of disbelief.

"Save it for the test," she giggled. "I just want to know more about this boyfriend," she said, lowering her voice. She pulled out her egg salad sandwich and took a big bite from it. I was still kinda huffing about Peachy's father's views and wasn't ready to talk boys now. Some men just had a way of cooling you off.

"What if I told you he was colored?" I blurted out. Peachy cleared her throat, nearly choking on the bread. She coughed into her fist and giggled again.

"Okay, right. Might as well tell me you are," she said, folding her wax paper and putting what she no longer had an appetite for back in her paper bag.

"And what if I was?" I asked her, showing a little more caution now. She stared at me a long time before bursting into laughter, stopping once to stare at me again and then continuing in her laughter.

"No, Peachy, what if I was Negro?" I asked again, still sounding serious. She stared at me a long time, her smile leaving her pretty face.

"A Negro in Wisconsin? What would you be hiding from?" She giggled while standing and gathering up her books. "And besides, then that would make your parents Negro, and I know that's not the case, because your father doesn't even allow coloreds in his store." She was telling me something I wasn't aware of.

"He doesn't?" I asked.

"No," she smarted off, cocking her head from side to side and twisting her hips.

Just then, the bell rang.

That night, while I lay in my bed, I prayed for God to forgive me for the things that were happening in my life. I prayed to be forgiven for the things that I had no control over and the things that I could change but wasn't brave enough to.

"I should have told Peachy that I'm a Negro," I said in an undertone.

Just then, my door cracked open. The size of the shadow left no doubt in my mind as to who it belonged to.

"Mr. Griffith?" I asked, before being shushed by his heavy hand over my mouth.

"Now you promised to call me Daddy, Emmy. You promised," he said, tugging at my blanket, which I gripped tighter now, holding on with all my might. He removed his hand, trusting that I wouldn't scream, and I didn't. I was beyond afraid, which actually put me in complete control of my senses. My mama had always taught me that a frightened woman who held in her fear had power, and I believed that.

"I want you to get out of my room, Mr. Griffith," I said firmly.

"Emmy, I need to sleep in here with you tonight," he said, shortening my name, yet saying it in a soft tone, while planting his large self on the edge of my bed.

I could smell the alcohol coming from him. I knew that smell well. Many a male visitor calling on my auntie at my mama's house had smelled as Mr. Griffith did tonight. I remember my mama telling me about my auntie's men callers.

"Never trust a man to hold you that can't even hold his drink," she'd told me. "He can't possibly be very strong, and I'd bet money, he'll drop you first," she'd added, with a wink.

I never understood her until that moment. Mr. Griffith was dropping Miss Greta and trying to pick up me.

"My bed is too small, Mr. Griffith, and so I think you need to go and get back in the bed with your wife," I urged.

He turned to me in the darkness of the room. With only the winter moon to show him the way to my face, he kissed me on my mouth. His kiss was nothing like Noah's. It was bitter and foul, and I gagged at his tongue's intrusion. It took both of my hands to remove his one heavy one as it laid on my breast.

"I thought you would be more appeasing, Emmy. I thought your people knew how to—"

"Mr. Griffith, please don't make me call Miss Greta," I begged.

"Who the hell do you think sent me in here?" he growled.

"I don't believe you," I said, squirming to escape his groping. I finally made it out of the bed. My hair was tossed all over my head, and I left it that way while I hung on to my gown for dear life as the big man started for me. I needed to be quick on my feet and not overly concerned with cuteness at that moment.

"You don't know what it's been like having a wife like Miss Greta. She's dead inside. She doesn't have a love for me anymore, Emmy," he said, moving in on me, pressing himself against me while smashing me against the wall. He kissed my neck as he raised my gown high above my hips. His hands ran down the length of my thighs. I could feel a hardness pressing against my leg. He wasn't Noah, and it just wasn't the same, and I knew then what was going to happen to me if I didn't think fast and move even faster.

"But I don't love you, either," I said, begging for reasonableness on his part.

Suddenly he froze. My words must have been like a bullet to his brain, because he stepped back from me, standing stiff for a moment, as if pondering what I had said.

"You're right, Emmy. Nobody loves me," he then said. His words were heavy and sad sounding. For a second I wanted to give the man a hug, I felt so bad for him, but there was no way I was gonna get close to him again. I slipped deeper into the darkness of the corner, silent, while Melvin Griffith slumped into the chair that sat by my door and wept like a baby.

After a minute or two, he was asleep. I grabbed up my blanket and went into the living room to sleep on the sofa.

Chapter 3

It was getting near Christmas, and everywhere people were humming familiar tunes. The kids my age were all caroling in the neighborhood. Peachy asked me to go along. "It's gonna be so much fun," she squealed while planning the night of caroling. She always spoke with so much excitement about little things.

"I believe you. I've just never done it," I confessed cautiously. Peachy's head cocked slightly to the side.

"You're joshing me, right?" she giggled. "The Griffiths seem like such happy and Christmassy people. I can't believe they don't let you carol. Is that why you didn't get to go last year? I thought it was just because you didn't know anybody."

"No, I've never gone to folks' houses, singing Christmas songs. I've never been allowed," I said again, blowing my hands, rubbing them together while trying to keep them warm. I didn't have any gloves. After the night in the room with Mr. Griffith, I'd noticed that my so-called mother had become rather cool toward me. Mrs. Griffith had stopped taking me to the store and allowing me to pick out the things I needed. My allowance was cut off completely. I was forced to live on a shoestring. It was getting hard. I was just glad she still allowed me to eat, although I did have to prepare my meals myself. Mr. Griffith, he seemed so sad every day that he was hard to look at.

Greta didn't ask me to join her at church anymore, as she had stopped attending herself. Without their knowledge, I had found one to attend . . . one of my own faith. It was on the colored side of town.

I had gotten brave one Sunday and had gone, only to find the members warm and accepting. It was strange being among my people after so long a time. I'd not seen a Negro face in over a year . . . since seeing the waiter on the train. They welcomed me in silent acceptance. It was as if they were just happy to be there . . . just happy to be. I had a feeling many of them were children of escaped slaves or maybe half Indians. I never knew why they were so warm and gentle, but I felt safe among them.

"Well, you're gonna go with me this year, aren't you?" Peachy asked, taking off one of her heavy gloves and handing it to me.

"What good is this, Peachy?" I asked her, looking it over.

"It's called better than nothing," she answered, grinning, blowing out a puff of smoke in the freezing air.

Peachy was such a good friend. I wanted to do something special for her . . . with her.

"Tell you what, Peachy. I'll go singing door to door if you go with me Sunday to church," I offered.

Gulping almost audibly, Peachy looked around. "Go to church? But it's not even Christmas yet."

"Yes, church. In colored town," I said, now adding to the offer, knowing that part would bring a reaction. Peachy's eyes popped open wide.

"What? Are you crazy?" she asked me. "What, you trying to get back at your folks for something they did or something?"

I thought about her words. They were an easy out to my situation. Blame it on the Griffiths, why not?

"No, Peachy, nothing like that. You go with me and I'll explain on the way," I negotiated.

I figured that would give me plenty of time to pray over this and get the strength I needed to tell my best friend the truth, at the risk of not having a best friend anymore. Although I was sworn to secrecy, something inside of me wanted to tell Peachy the truth. That I was a Negro.

"Deal. Now go ask your folks about tonight. Jerry and Keith are gonna go, too. This is gonna be so much fun," Peachy squealed, squeezing my ungloved hand, giggling. She was so very cute and easily excited about everything that I had to laugh, too. At our age, we both should have found life exciting and fun. But for me, it was only through Peachy's eyes that I found joy.

I didn't need to ask the Griffiths about going out that night with Peachy and the rest of our group of friends, as later that evening Mrs. Griffith went to play bridge with her friends and Mr. Griffith retired to the big chair, with a bottle of Jack Daniels.

Peachy sang her heart out while holding on to Jerry's arm, still wearing the one glove of the set we shared. Jerry allowed this show of affection, stating that it was the season to give and show love. We all knew what he meant by that. Keith, on the other hand, just stared at me, standing close but not too close. He was so silly, in my opinion.

When I returned home, I thought Mr. Griffith was asleep in the large chair, which had been his resting place for days, so I attempted to creep past him, but he awoke.

"Emmy," he called to me. I froze—my heart beating like a drum.

"Yes, Mr. Griffith?" I said.

"I love you very much," he said, sounding sober.

I turned and looked at him now. His normally well-groomed beard was tangled, and his hair a mess. He'd lost weight, I could see it in his face, and his pretty blue eyes were dull and full of tears. I wanted to cry just looking at him. I wanted to say that I loved him just so he would feel better. But I couldn't. I didn't want any problems.

"I know," was all I said, and then I went on into my room.

I had only been sleep a short time, but my slumber went deep. My dreams had taken me to a place that included violent scenes from my hometown. I saw Noah there in the dream. He was coming toward me through a crowd of angry people, all fighting the nothingness. I called out to him, louder and louder; then suddenly, a shot rang out, piercing the hum of angry voices.

I jolted awake, nearly leaping from my bed. Hesitating only long enough to slip quickly into my house shoes and robe, I ran from my room. However, what I found I could have waited a lifetime to see; it was truly a sight that would stay with me forever.

It was Mr. Griffith sitting there in that large chair, with what was left of his face, a mangled twist of hair, blood, and brain matter, and Mrs. Griffith dropping a pistol down onto his lap.

My screams cut the air like a sharp razor, and I'm sure that brought the neighbors running faster than the sound of the gunshot, as a neighbor woman burst through the front door.

"What's happened?" asked the neighbor woman as she began to push me back into my room. I didn't want to fight her, but she was hurting me, pushing me hard and rough.

"Stop," I snapped at her.

"Now, Emmy, do what you're told and get back to bed," she fussed at me. "You don't need to see what's going on here." She was acting as if she was in charge of me.

I looked around her to see what I could see and caught a glimpse of Mrs. Griffith covering Mr. Griffith with a white sheet, and perhaps I was wrong, but a piece of paper that wasn't there before was there now—at his feet.

The woman couldn't hold me back anymore. I pushed past her into the living room.

Mrs. Griffith stood still and pale. Her arms were folded tight against her chest, and her bloodstained hand was over her mouth as she stood staring at the big man now covered with the sheet. I looked over at the covered Mr. Griffith and saw only the blood staining the linen and the blood pooled by his feet, soaking the note. There was a lot of blood.

"Mrs. Grif . . . I mean, Mother, what did you do?" I asked, stumbling badly over my words and my feet as I rushed to her side. I reached for her to comfort her, only to have her recoil from me as if I were a leper. "Mother?" I wondered why she pulled away from me.

"You, harlot." Her words were said with a coldness that froze me.

"What is that?" I asked, as I had not heard the word used in everyday speech. I'd heard it only in church, and I didn't think that evil of a reference applied to me.

"This is all your fault!" she said. And, with those words, she slapped me hard across the face, leaving a stickiness on my cheek. I knew it was blood as her hands were covered with it. The neighbor woman came between us.

Mrs. Griffith was accusing me of awful acts with Mr. Griffith and promising me that I would get the same if I said a word. The neighbor woman began shaming me off to hell.

Within seconds, it seemed, the house filled with people, and my mind scattered in a million directions as all the voices blended into a mesh of angry sound.

Dr. Graham was there now. He lived only a few houses down. He was trying to calm everyone down.

"Someone needs to call the police," I heard one of our neighbors say, and I grew afraid at that thought. With Mrs. Griffith suddenly acting as if she didn't know me, perhaps she would allow me to be arrested for murdering Mr. Griffith—or something strange like that.

"He killed himself!" someone screamed.

"He killed himself," I heard myself say over and over again.

Before I hit the front door on my way outside, I could have sworn I saw Mrs. Griffith smile at me— a kind of evil smile, which didn't set all that well in my mind. It would take years to get that evil grin out of my dreams.

Suddenly, in the crowd of people pushing their way into the Griffiths' house and onto their front lawn, I saw Peachy. She had come, and was I ever so relieved to see her. "Peachy," I called, feeling nearly out of breath just running to the sidewalk to meet her.

"Emma, folks are sayin' your mama shot your daddy tonight," she said, her face showing total fear and confusion. She then, noticing the blood on my face, spit on the sleeve of her coat and began scrubbing at it.

"No, no . . . Miss Greta wouldn't have shot Mr. Griffith," I said, my words coming out before I could catch them. "Mr. Griffith shot hisself." I flinched at the roughing up Peachy was giving my cheek.

"Why you calling your mama and daddy that?" she asked me, holding my shoulders, trying to keep me from shaking. I think the shock was coming in on me, as I shook like a leaf on a windy day. The vision of Mr. Griffith's head, or rather what was left of it, filled my mind and turned my stomach. And that wicked, wicked grin . . .

"I'm gonna be sick, Peachy," I told her.

"Come on," she said, taking me by the arm and leading me down the street, toward her house.

Just then, the officer called for us to stop where we were. He needed to ask me some questions. "I can't talk. I'm gonna be sick," I told him. Unable to hold on to my stomach any longer, I vomited.

I remember thinking at that very moment, before soiling the shoes of that tall officer, I was sure glad he thought I was white.

Chapter 4

Spring, 1953

I hadn't seen Peachy since the night Mr. Griffith . . .
well, the night of the incident. Spring was upon us now,
and I was a senior in high school, set to graduate in just
a few months. Mrs. Griffith had not even pressed me to
return to classes once the quarter started back up after
the start of the year, and I didn't feel in a rush to go.
She seemed so needy, and I so wanted to fulfill her
needs. None of her friends had been by to see her. I
have to believe that once the news of Mr. Griffith's un-
timely demise hit the local paper, it filled many with
suspicions. Rumors were flying; I heard the mumbles
in the market when I would do the shopping. After that
night, the Griffiths' store had been closed.

I'm never going to be sure if that eager detective
that came by every evening just refused to believe that
a robust man like Melvin Griffith would have ever allowed sorrow and sadness to bring him to such an un-
godly decision as suicide. Or was it the loose ends of
the whole thing? The typewritten note; the gun,
which had none of his fingerprints on it; or Greta

Griffith's bloody hands? No one may ever know because, as for my thoughts on the whole thing, I kept them to myself.

"But we're gonna get to the bottom of what happened here," the detective said to me, with a threat in his words. And, with that order, the police went through the Griffiths' house with a fine-tooth comb, looking for what, I hadn't a clue. But, apparently, after one of their visits, they found it.

What a very strange turn of events for Greta Griffith, she being arrested for the murder of her husband. They didn't believe a word of what she had to tell them about her husband's depression being at the root of his suicide. They believed less the excuse of unrequited love between Mr. Griffith and some mysterious younger woman. I remembered asking myself what it all meant and if it really mattered. Things had gotten back to normal in a way after his death, and so I'd figured it would just be me and Greta Griffith forever living in that house, but no, they took about two months investigating all there was to know about the Griffiths, and that led them to arrest her for murder.

I remember thinking that it was very poor timing when the coppers took her away. I remember thinking, *What poor timing. We have cookies in the oven.*

Peachy had heard the news about Miss Greta's arrest, and risking all popularity with our peers, she appeared at the Griffiths' front door later that night.

Surprisingly enough, no one had come to get me or move me to another home. Perhaps they thought I was older, or perhaps they didn't care.

"I knew they were going to charge her with murder," Peachy said as we shared a few of the cookies that Miss

Greta and I had been making that afternoon—before the police came and took her away.

I looked around, hoping that no one had heard us talking about it. It seemed as though there were spies lurking about. I felt watched and nervous suddenly. Without Mrs. Griffith absorbing all the guilt, I was now catching some of it.

"But she didn't kill him," I protested. I think, inside, I wanted to believe it.

"They're calling her the Black Widow," Peachy said in a low voice. "They're saying she killed him for the store and for a lot of other reasons." She looked off, with instant regret over her words.

"What other reasons?" I asked her, trying to bring her face back around to mine. Finally, I just grabbed her chin and pulled it my way.

"You never told me you were adopted," Peachy said now, her eyes rimming with tears.

My stomach reacted. I sat my cookie down. It was so hard to take that girl serious, and especially now, as she wore a thick milk mustache. I motioned with my sleeve for her to imitate me in cleaning off her top lip.

"What are they sayin', Peachy?" I asked.

Peachy absently wiped her milk mustache. "You know that Keith's father is a lawyer. Well, Keith said that the Griffiths adopted you and that . . ." She hesitated. "I don't believe them, of course," Peachy said, now almost choking on the words. "And that's not all. They're saying that Mrs. Griffith told Mrs. Baker that you and Mr. Griffith were doing things that, well . . ." Peachy stopped speaking as her face turned from peachy to more the color of a tomato.

"Mr. Griffith and me never did anything," I balked, now standing and wringing my hands. The two of us were silent for a moment, and I could tell Peachy was working her hardest to send me a positive vibe, but it wasn't helping at all. I was scared to death.

"Peachy, what's gonna happen?" I finally asked her as she stared at me, no doubt noting that the only part of what she had said that I had denied was the immorality with Mr. Griffith.

"Emmy . . . Are you a Negro?" she asked me, coming closer to me, as if examining me closely. I pushed her back a little.

"Peachy . . ." I said, laughing a little, nervously hoping that just by doing that she would stop this third degree.

"Answer me. Is that why you wanted me to go with you to colored town? Is that why you—"

"Yes," I finally exploded, unable to hold it in any longer. "Now are you happy? Go on now. Stop being my friend . . . Go tell everybody. I'm sure they've all been waiting to hear the truth. It's all right. I didn't plan to go back to school, anyway." I started feeling the heat of my tears as they seared my face. I waited for the mocking to come from Peachy, but instead, using her bare hand, she wiped the tears from my face.

"It's going to be all right," she said, smiling at me.

The next morning, the police at the door awakened me. Again, the detective needed to question me. Only this time he needed to question me down at the station house.

When we arrived down at the station, the detective started right in on me. "We're starting to think that perhaps you and Greta Griffith might have plotted together to kill Melvin," he said, pointing a short, thick finger in my face.

"What are you saying?" I asked, trying to hold in my panic.

"Greta confessed to killing her husband," the detective barked, blowing cigarette smoke in my face. "But we think she's just protecting someone," he added.

"She confessed?" I asked, certain that confusion was showing on my face.

"You scared?" he asked me, now getting real close to me. "Is she protecting you perhaps? I know sometimes women get kinda attached to things they shouldn't, and it causes them to act foolishly." Suddenly, I realized he knew about me. Greta had told him about me, and no doubt, her reasons for killing her husband did, in fact, have to do with me. I wasn't stupid; it was true. She'd found a way to blame the whole thing on me.

My mother had warned me about unhappy people. "Misery loves company," she would say.

I don't remember much else of that day, except the face of that detective and threatening words. Yes, I was now afraid as I did not intend to keep Greta Griffith company in jail. They had no grounds to hold me, so I got to go home. But the detective promised me he would be coming around in a day or two.

Later that night, and with the help of Peachy, I formulated my plan of escape. I don't know why I felt as if flight would be my best bet at that juncture, but somewhere deep inside my heart, I knew, "Emerald, it's best you getta gettin'."

Neither Peachy nor I had all the money I needed to get back to Shreveport, but I knew I could at least get closer than I was now. I needed to find help among my own kind. Remembering my mother telling me about my father being somewhere in St. Louis, I reasoned that, surely, he would help me get home. I had just about enough to get there, so I bought the ticket. I'd find him; I was certain of it. I prayed.

I told Peachy that this would probably be the last time I saw her. "I'll think about you often, Peachy," I said to her at the bus depot, standing outside the loading bus. It hurt my heart to leave her, but I was confident that she would be all right. At that moment, I was more confident of her life's successes than my own.

"Think about me? What good will that do me?" she asked, again giving way to tears. I held her in a tight squeeze.

"It's better than nothing," I assured her, causing a little chuckle to come out of her.

Chapter 5

I'd never braved the streets alone after dark before, but tonight, with my suitcase in hand, I found myself in St. Louis, Missouri, in the heart of the ghetto streets. The cab driver thought me crazy for having him bring me here, but if I was ever going to get home, I needed to find my father. Foolishly, I just felt that if I found him, he would somehow just know me and help me get home. Back home everybody knew everybody, and all you had to say was, "I'm Maybelle Jackson's daughter," and poof, so, yes, I figured it would be as easy as that, and I would be back by my mother's side.

Never would I have thought this part of town would so alive with sights, sounds, and most of all . . . color. I suppose I was showing nearly as much prejudice as the white folks there in Wisconsin, because I was truly hesitant and eager to get out of the nightlife I found there in the hustle and bustle of the snow-covered streets of the colored people's neighborhood.

It wasn't long before I came upon a church. Standing out front, I could hear the music and the singing.

The choir was lifting the roof with hymns I had only heard in my recent dreams. It warmed my soul.

Stepping on the concrete of that church's steps and opening those doors, I could almost hear my knees knocking. I'd not seen this many of my people in one place in a long time. And, to my heart's disconcertment, it felt almost foreign to me. I was hoping that once I went inside, I would feel differently.

The usher rushed quickly over to me, and I was seated as the preacher was up there, grinning broadly, showing his gold teeth. A chemical process had slicked down his hair, and his diction was extravagant. He had just begun his sermon, with a booming voice that rattled my bones. I must admit, his words had me jumping, from his powerful emphasis on hellfire and damnation awaiting the liar. Why did I feel so much guilt? And why I felt instantly so out of place, I could not explain, either. Perhaps it was the way the members were looking at me. The women looked at me with so much animosity; and the men, with so much curiosity behind their wide grins.

As the choir sang, I looked around, noticing now that all the women overtly ignored me after giving me a once-over, fanning their fans hard and fast, while all the fine, strong men were eyeing me up and down, no doubt wondering about the motives of this young *white* girl sitting here in the house of their Lord. They were looking at me with both apprehension and lust. I saw it in their eyes. It was nothing like the way the blacks in Wisconsin had viewed me. These eyes were the eyes of prejudice and hate.

I saw and felt things I had never seen before in the church, and I suddenly wanted to leave.

Had I changed that much in a few months' time? Remembering my mama's warning about *my time* and how men would start reacting to me, I supposed *my time* was upon me . . . whatever that meant. "And, well, I don't like it. This is not the place for it," I heard myself say before I got up to leave.

At the door, one of the young men stopped me. He was a rich tone of brown, almost like a piece of chocolate, the kind you savor in your mouth after you take a bite.

"Problem, my white sister?" he asked before I felt my eyes rip him. "The Lord accepts your kind here, too."

"My kind? You don't know anything about my kind," I said, growing angry and pushing past him and on outside. He followed me out.

"Look, there's no need to get all upset," he said, keeping up with my quickening pace. "I just dropped in for a few minutes myself," he admitted. "Sometimes the Rev gets kinda carried away, sending all us fun-lovin' folks off to hell all the damn time." He chuckled. His laughter was infectious, but I fought catching the bug. He'd not earned my good side yet.

Not knowing where I was going, I just walked. All I wanted was to get away from him.

"Look here, my white sista. You came to us," he said, now causing me to slam on my brakes, so to speak.

"I am colored, just like you," I snapped, grabbing his hand and comparing it to mine. "Can't you see it? Why can't you see it?" I yelled, growing hysterical, slamming his hand down to his side. "My mother is a Negro. I'm Negro!" I cried, pulling at my hair, which was tightly curling at the roots from the damp weather. I was exhausted, hungry, in need of a hot bath, and making no sense at all, I was sure, as the boy looked me dead in the eye and then burst into laughter.

"Yeah, okay," he said. "I'm bitin', and I don't even care why you wanna be." He snatched my bag from me against my protest.

"Where you stayin'?" he asked.

"I don't know," I answered angrily.

"Come on, my white . . . uh, wannabe colored sista," he said, still chuckling a little. "Look, I don't know what your game is, but tell you what, you might wanna get out of this hea side of town before it gets too much later and you can't get out. You know what I mean?" His tone grew a little more serious as he licked his full lips while looking around. Yes, he reminded me of a piece of sweet chocolate.

"Take me back to the church then," I told him, sounding a little bossy. But I was tired, and I needed someone to understand me.

"What's the church gonna do?" he asked me.

"The reverend'll help me get to my family."

"Your family? Ooooh, one of women in the church works for your family or something like that? You looking for—"

"No," I pleaded, before finally realizing that I was gonna get nowhere with this boy. "Yes, yes, that's it. I've run off from my folks, and I'm looking for the woman that used to take care of me when I was a child," I said, speaking the way I had learned to speak in Wisconsin over this last year. "I'm sure she'll take me in," I added. "Her last name was Hutchinson." I'd never met my father, but this would be as good a time as any, I reckoned. "I'll even take a Jackson if you have one," I said, thinking that maybe my mother might have a relative or two in these parts.

"Hutchinson? Ain't no Hutchinsons live around here, and way too many Jacksons to sort through right now. Where you from?" he asked me as we headed slowly back to the church.

"Shrev . . . Texas," I said. "Dallas. Do you know where that is?" I asked, lying and showing a little sarcasm in my tone. He glared at me. I had pushed the wrong button now.

"Yes, I do. And this is St. Louis. Do you know where that is?" he asked me, showing the same sarcasm.

He had won this battle without much fight. I didn't know where I was, and he knew it. Before I knew it, we had returned to the church and met with the minister, whose sanctuary placard identified him as Reverend Bickel.

"Glad you came home again, my fair-skinned sista," the Reverend Bickel said to me, with a quick wink. I couldn't help but smile. He looked funny and made me feel good inside. His wink seemed more out of habit than anything, and it made me want to laugh.

"Dad, this is . . ." the boy began his introduction. I looked at him sideways. The reverend was his father. After all the mean things he had said outside the church, too. Boy, was I glad I had not spoken my mind about the reverend's sermon.

"What is your name?" the boy asked.

"Daryl, you drug her hea without even knowing her name?" the reverend said.

"I didn't drag her anywhere," Daryl snapped, showing irritation. "What's your name, chile?" Daryl asked again.

"Em . . . Sarah," I lied.

Don't ask me why I lied, but there was something deep inside of me that forced it from my mouth, and once out, I knew there would be no turning back from it.

"Well, Miss Sarah," the reverend greeted me customarily.

"You can just call me Sarah," I corrected politely. It was bad enough that it wasn't my name. I sure wasn't going to have this grown man adding any supremacy to it. He smiled as if happy about my humility.

"So, Sarah, who be your people?" Reverend Bickel asked me.

"The Hutchinsons or Jacksons. She hasn't made up her mind," Daryl answered for me. "She's looking for some folks named one of them names," he added, throwing his father into a moment of deep contemplation over the dilemma.

About that time one of the women from the choir came from a back room. She appeared to have just refreshed herself and was placing her hat back on her head of thick curls. Upon spying me in conference with the reverend and Daryl in the sanctuary, she frowned.

"Who is this?" she asked smartly, her finger pointing at me, her other hand landing firmly on her hip. I unconsciously grabbed on to Daryl's hand. He must have noticed, as his grip tightened.

"Hur name is Say-rah," the reverend said. His diction was rougher than when he had spoken before the congregation.

"Uh-huh. And, Sarah, can we be of service to you this evening?" the woman asked.

"This is my mother," Daryl said. "Mrs. Betty Bickel." I sighed, now relieved, and outstretched my hand, at which she wrinkled her nose. At first, I was intimidated by the woman; however, the longer I stood there with my hand out, the more she reminded me of my aunt Rebecca, a headstrong, proud, admirable Negro woman— angry at the oppression of her ancestors and carrying the weight of the world on her shoulders. My aunt had taught me pride, too. She'd taught me to stand strong in the face of the enemy. I would not lower my hand until this woman either spit in it or shook it; whichever happened first, I was ready for.

"Sarah," she nodded, finally shaking my hand reluctantly.

"I'm wondering if you know of a place where I might stay the night until I locate my family," I said to her.

"Here?" the woman asked, her voice peaking a bit.

"It's okay, Mama . . . Sarah says she's Negro," Daryl taunted as I watched his mother's eyes dart from Daryl to her husband and then back to me.

"Well, praise the Lawd," Reverend Bickel exclaimed, flashing his gold front teeth in a wide grin.

I could see the woman, Betty Bickel, looking me over now, examining me from where she stood. She believed that I was colored, I could tell. She'd apparently seen many Creole people in St. Louis, but that didn't make my presence any easier for her to take.

Chapter 6

Perhaps it was the way that well-used ashtray filled with burnt filtered butts of cigarettes tipped with bright red lipstick rested on top of a Holy Bible that first struck me when I entered into their home.

The Bickel house was one of the largest homes I'd ever known a Negro to own. Apparently, the church had financed it to also serve as a hotel for people passing through. It spoke of good living and much materialism.

Maybe Betty Bickel wanted me to see this part of her before seeing anything else in the community. Perhaps she was setting down the rules for me right here, right now. I don't know. But I heard them loud and clear. . . .

Don't think too much of yourself, "high yella gal," because you're just a bug to be smashed under my heel! And don't get too comfortable, either. You are just passing through—remember that.

"Here's where you can sleep," Betty said, instead of those thoughts that I was sure she had.

She led me to a small room off the back porch. It wasn't as warm as the rest of the house and was not well lit, either. I couldn't believe it was one of the normal rooms used for guests. When she clicked on the small lamp that sat on the little table next to the small bed, I could see this was her sewing room: there were piles of fabric on the chairs near the wall, and her sewing needs were hanging on little nails bent in the wall. But this room was better than a jail cell, and that's what waited for me back in Milwaukee. I believed that. In my mind, my days of living white were over, and I needed to get used to that thought right here and right now. I had messed it up for myself and felt terrible that I couldn't live up to my mother's last wishes any better than this.

"Thank you, ma'am," I said to Mrs. Bickel, catching her right before she closed the door behind her, leaving without so much as a good night. She turned back to me, with dark eyes that glowed against the dim light. Her lips curved now into a wicked smile.

"Look here, chile, you gone be leaving come tomorrah," she said. "I don't want you here, but seeings as how I'm a preacher's wife, I have to do this good deed tonight. But I knows about your kind. I've heard about your kind all my life. You bring evil. Now I'm not superstitious, because the good Lawd watches over me!" she ranted, raising her hands and voice as if about to break into song. "But you stay away from my family, you evil she-devil you," she snapped, pointing her finger at me.

I felt my eyes blinking quickly as my brain could not process her words as fast as I was taking them in.

"What . . . ?" I began.

"Stay away from my boy," she said again, her words said with a tight grin and a shake of her head. "Not in the arms of a foreign woman let him lay!" she added, misquoting scripture. "You Hittite woman," she growled, shaking her head again as she continued to give me a holy cursing. She was a hard woman to read, and so I didn't try. She was convinced that she understood herself, and that was all that mattered—I suppose.

When the light went out, I attempted to pray. I needed to ask God why I was here. Had the last three days since leaving Wisconsin been worth the effort? I asked God why I had been so naive as to think that he would simply lead me to my family, my home, back to Noah without a struggle. "With all the lies I've told and lived, how could you want to help me, Lord?" I prayed.

"But, God, just answer me this, do the Hutchinsons really exist?" I asked before ending and turning over, tucking the thin blankets around me, and utilizing my coat for extra warmth.

Chapter 7

Daryl peeked in my room early the next morning, letting in the wandering aroma of breakfast cooking. I hoped with all hope that Betty Bickel had made enough for me, too.

"Wake up, sleepyhead," Daryl said, grinning broadly at me from the doorway. He was friendly, but he was not Noah.

"What time is it?" I asked.

"Where do you have to go?" he asked me, sounding full of play as he came all the way into the small room. I pulled the blanket tight around me, seeings as how he had no respect for my privacy. And I was only wearing my slip.

"Is it true?" he asked me.

"Is what true?" I asked him, stifling a yawn.

"About girls like you," he said.

"What about girls like me?" I asked again, showing my innocence. Finally, he shook his head, as if too embarrassed to continue the questioning.

Just then, I heard his father call, and Daryl hurried back to the door.

"Get on up so we can eat breakfast," he ordered me

before slamming the door closed in his guilt-ridden haste to leave.

Betty Bickel ran a woman's clothing store in the heart of the community as well as this church-funded hostel. Apparently, between that and the Reverend's takings from the flock's contributions, they lived quite well.

Daryl was a year older than I was and played a trumpet.

"At the juke joint downtown," Daryl told me later that afternoon as he polished up the instrument. "My folks don't know about all that, though. I'm thinking that if I keep playing, soon I'll be discovered and end up in the Big Apple, maybe even in a bop band, playing some cool jazz with that cat Miles Davis," Daryl went on, sounding excited. "You ever heard of him?"

"No, but I would like to hear you play," I urged, getting caught up in his excitement. He looked at me out of the corner of his eye. I'm sure I looked different from the night before, as I had bathed and eaten and was a lot friendlier now. I'd even combed my hair, and it hung softly along my shoulders and down my arms.

"Okay," he agreed eagerly. "Tonight then. I bug out after dark. My folks are usually down there at the church and never seem to miss me when I cut outta there halfway through all that bullshit my father is spitting out, long as I make it back before it's over." His lowered voice let me know that perhaps he'd been missed on occasion and had paid the price for his disobedience. "It's cool." I had no such restrictions and so was game to go with him. "I had just come back when you slid your little self in there last night," Daryl told me.

"Really now? And here I was thinking you were a good little church boy," I teased. It must have sounded like flirting, as he licked his full lips and winked at me.

"Nah, I'm not good nor little . . . if you get my meaning." He winked. I didn't know what he meant but foolishly giggled, anyway.

Who knew if I would still be in this house another night? Who cared? So, yes, I had thrown caution to the wind. Just the thought of not having a home or place to call home gave me a light-headed, airy feeling. I'd never felt so free.

It was nearly time for Betty Bickel to come home. She'd made it abundantly clear that one night and one meal was all I was to have in her home. So I headed to the small room to toss my things in my bag and ready myself to leave. While I did, Daryl watched me.

"What?" I asked, unconsciously flipping my hair over my shoulder. It had grown long and clearly reached my waist. I had taken to twisting it up on my head, the way Greta had instructed me to, but today I let it hang. *Why not?* I thought to myself.

"Is it true?" he asked me again.

This time I knew I had to answer him. Getting in his face, I pulled on his collar, pretending to rough him up. "What are you talking about?" I asked, sounding almost like that cop who had questioned me. He chuckled and took my hands in his.

"You are so pretty. You are like a dream," he said to me now as our faces were close to each other.

"Yeah, a nightmare," I joked, thinking about myself as a jinx. God had given me no sign of what I was to do or where I was to go. I was living my worst nightmare— well, one of them, anyway.

"No, don't say that. My mother . . ." he began.

"What?" I asked right before his lips met mine in a kiss. His lips felt familiar. . . .

"Noah?" I heard my voice ask in a whisper. Maybe

God had answered me and had sent Noah to me in the form of Daryl to protect me. Maybe with Noah wearing the locket, he could will himself to me in another form. I tried to reason every way that I could on how to make Daryl, Noah, because the kiss felt so good. But when my eyes opened, I gazed into Daryl's pools of polluted coffee, not the pure eyes of Noah. These eyes were not as innocent as Noah's were, and despite the heat his kiss had caused and the tremor I felt in my belly, there was no purity in Daryl's soul.

"You talking the Bible to me now," he said and smiled, walking me backward until I fell onto the bed, with him on top of me, holding my hands apart high above my head.

"No, I was thinking of—," I attempted to explain, but his kiss interrupted me. His hungry passion caught me off guard. He wasn't Mr. Griffith, and I didn't feel sick to my stomach, although my belly reacted to his touch—quivering, tickling me, causing me to giggle. As he rubbed on my legs and my breast and kissed me, that small, cold room began to heat up. It was almost too hard to breathe, as he covered me completely, nearly smothering me with his weight and winter clothing.

"You're not like other girls, Sarah," he said now, breathing heavily after a few more kisses on my neck.

I don't know what I was thinking by allowing that moment to happen, getting as carried away as I did. But as soon as I felt his hardness coming through his slacks, I knew the moment had gone too far. Daryl's desire for me was even more evident than Mr. Griffith's had been. Daryl was young and virile, and he wanted to make me feel the way Noah had in his room . . . in his bed the day we married.

Suddenly, I thought about Noah and the day we said our good-byes. I had dreamed of that day often and missed the feeling Noah's body had caused to come up in me. Could I allow Daryl to have my love when I knew it belonged to Noah? No. I was not going to betray my Noah this way. I attempted to get up, but Daryl slammed me back on the bed. I tried to move but couldn't budge. Daryl was much stronger than Mr. Griffith had been, too.

"I don't love you," I told him, hoping to stop him as easily as I had Mr. Griffith, but instead, Daryl removed my panties and smiled at me.

"Like I said, you're very different from other girls, Sarah."

"Stop . . . I'm married. I'm married!" I screamed.

"Yeah, just like you're a Negro and just like you came home with us to find your family. All lies, Sarah. You want this. You've probably wanted a colored boy in your panties for a long time, and now, baby, you got one," he said, growling as if angry all of a sudden. I know I was getting pretty angry. I wanted him to get off me; I wanted my underwear back. I wanted to get out of there. With one hand, he held me down, and with the other, he unzipped his pants.

Suddenly, the door burst open, and Betty Bickel added to the heat already in the room. Only this heat was the heavy, angry heat breathed out of her nostrils as she stormed in.

"You whorish Hittite woman! I told you to stay away from my sweet boy!" she screamed. I jumped from the bed, grabbing quickly at my underwear. I looked around for Daryl, who had been slammed against the wall by his mother's unnatural strength. He about lost consciousness from hitting his head so hard. I screamed when she next grabbed my hair and wrapped it around her hand and began slapping my face, hard.

This was insanity, I thought now. I couldn't just stand there and let this woman beat on me. Her son was about to rape me, and here I was, being made the evil one! I thought of my mother's words and wished she was there so I could get a full understanding of what had just happened. But there was no time for that. I caught Mrs. Bickel's hand and bit it, causing her to yelp and let go of me. I snatched my coat and suitcase, but not before she recovered from her first fit and started the next, coming at me with scissors in her hand.

"God, am I gonna die today?" I yelled out. "What have I done?"

Almost as if touched by the angel of mercy, Mrs. Bickel, instead of stabbing me in the heart with those sharp scissors, grabbed my hair again and cut it. Jagged, wild hacks at my hair, uneven, angry snips. Daryl then grabbed his mother's arms as my severed locks fell. I had no time to grieve as I ran from the room.

I ran a long time once I cleared the Bickels' property. I know many people saw me, as I heard voices and calls for me to stop and even someone asking if they could help the apparently lost white girl—me. But no one could help me. I was a displaced soul.

Just then, a large car pulled up, and a woman leaned out of the window.

"Gal, what's happenin' to you? And what are you doing out here?" she asked me, noting my beat-up appearance. I'm sure she thought I had just escaped a near-death experience—which, in my opinion, I had.

The car door swung open, and I climbed in with the strange, wild-eyed woman, with the curly hair that bounced in her eyes and the manly clothes and cowboy boots. I then noticed I no longer had my suitcase. As I took a quick accounting of myself, our eyes met for a second, and I knew she would help me. I then laid my head against the window and closed my eyes, surrendering to the rescue.

When I awoke, we were pulling into the driveway of an old, colonial-looking house. She nudged me.

"Come on. Let's get you cleaned up and see what's what." Her diction was deeply seated in Texas.

Chapter 8

"What's your name?" the woman asked me as I washed my face, avoiding the mirror. I didn't want to see the butcher job Betty Bickel had done on my hair.

"I'm Molly," she said, standing in the doorway of the bathroom, with her hands crossed over her chest. I glanced over the woman; she had a cute face, reminding me of the cheerleaders at my school in Wisconsin. She stared at me with her clear blue eyes and pulled back her dishwater blond hair.

"I'm Em . . . Sar . . ." I sighed, heavily rubbing my head now. What did it matter anymore?

"I'm Emerald Jackson," I said to her as she stepped closer to me, holding up what was left of my long tresses, examining them, comparing them to the short hair that covered most of my head.

"What happened to you?" she asked. Feeling my eyes roll, I sighed again and gulped a handful of water from my hand. She handed me a towel.

"Pretty girl like you out roaming around in that neighborhood. . . . Did you get shanghaied or what?"

"No. I had gotten into town and needed a place to stay and, well. . . . It turned out to be a mistake,"

I answered. My words sounded vacant to even my own ears. I was truly lost . . . I believed that now.

"Well, dealing with them folks is always a mistake," she snapped, with a scowl. I just stared at her, wondering what to say next. Did I tell her to her face that I, too, was one of *those folks* and miss out on maybe another hot meal, a bath, and a bed?

"Look, I'm not a stupid woman. I'm blunt and to the point. I like honesty, although I'll lie in a minute to make a dollar." She cackled, slapping her leg before continuing. "You must be in some kinda trouble, right?" she asked, though her words were said more as a statement of fact. "I don't care what it is unless it involves a baby or the law," she went on after reaching in her closet and after sizing me up, handing me a denim shirt and a pair of boyish-looking Levi's. "You're about my size." The silence now required me to answer.

"No baby," I said.

"Good. Don't need no half-breed interfering with what could be a prosperous plan," she went on, while circling me, looking me up and down. I guess she figured I was white and, being in the black community, would give birth to a mixed baby. "I assume you don't have family, I mean none that care, or you wouldn't be roaming the streets," she said, her finger to her lip, as if her plan, whatever it was, was coming to fruition with each circle she made around me.

Was I the answer to some crazy dream she'd had?

She was unnerving me.

"You say your name is Emerald?" she asked, now showing her puzzlement. I nodded slowly. She was silent for a time and then shrugged. "Go figure. Must be on account of them eyes of yours." She cackled again and then motioned for me to follow her into the kitchen. She showed me to a chair. "Well, Emerald," she said, reaching for a large pair of scissors. I hesitated, notably. "Oh, gal, I'm not gonna hurt you. I'm just gonna even out that mop that's left of your hair," she said. Molly's voice now took on a little pity.

I'm sure the sight of my beautiful hair butchered as it was would hurt anyone at that moment, especially realizing that evening it out would mean cutting it right below my ears in a bop cut and giving me bangs—the likes of which I had never had nor desired to have in my life. I looked like a beatnik when Molly was finished. She smiled at the cutting job she had done.

"I used to cut my husband's hair before he died. Sure, he ain't never had a mane like this, but you get me. I'm just saying I do know what I'm doing," she said proudly, spinning the scissors like a pistol and then blowing on the tip of them. I had to laugh at the funny woman and worry at the same time. With all that had occurred in the last year of my life, I wondered what she would ask in return for the kindness she'd shown me today.

I stood. "Well, Miss Molly, I think I'm gonna get going. I thank you for helping me out of that jam and all. I—"

"Hold your horses there, li'l lady," she said, cutting me off and holding up her hand to stop me.

"Look, I don't have any money, I don't have"—I looked around myself—"I don't have anything now." I kept a handle on my growing emotions. I hadn't thought about Daryl since bursting from that house, and now the vision of his face hovering over me came back full on.

"You need a job?" she asked me flatly.

"Job?"

"That's what I said, and I don't think I stutter." She cackled.

"Why me?"

"Why anybody?" she said, putting the scissors down. Suddenly, she, too, appeared reflective. She looked up to the ceiling and then down to the floor. "Today I was driving around, feeling sorry for myself. Here I am, a woman in my prime, and already I've lost a lot of my will, ya know." She began squinting her eyes tight, as if holding back tears. "I'm a widow at my young age. I married this old codger, and well, frankly, I thought I was pretty set. But, no, he died, and even then I figured . . . circle of life, ya know, I'll still be all right. But then I came up here from Dallas because this state here, of Missouri, is where my beloved was from. This is where his will was read and . . ." Suddenly she scowled. "And contested by his ass of a son, Brent!" she growled and then stabbed the counter with the scissors. They stood on end.

"I don't know much about wills," I began cautiously, not wanting to upset the woman in any way.

"Well, honey, you stick with me and you'll find out about 'em," she snipped. "Anyway, even this house, this house belongs to Brent now, and he wants me to give it to him," she said, fanning her arms out dramatically as if the house—the one she had just stabbed with sharp scissors—meant everything to her. "He wants everything that my husband had except a few measly dollars. He even wants my ranch. But that bastard can't have my hard work . . . and that's what that ranch is, my hard fuckin' work," she barked. I flinched at her language but still tried to listen to the point she was making.

She went on. "He tells me that if I can get the ranch to turn a profit, then he'll let me keep it. If not, then he wants to turn it into some kinda shopping center. Can you believe it? As if people are gonna come way out to the middle of nowhere to visit a J. C. Penney or Sears and Roebuck. He's insane."

"That sounds awful," I said, thinking for the first time about Melvin Griffith and the possibility of his will. I wondered for a second who would now own his things, seeings as how Greta was surely gonna fry for killing him and they had no *real* children.

"So I was driving around, like I said. And it came to me, Molly, just pull up your bootstraps and work the damn ranch yourself. Get you some investors, and build it into a showplace!" she said, her eyes growing wide with imagination.

I stood, still wondering where picking up a she-devil like me on the side of the road came into this dream. Unconsciously, I ran my fingers over my hair, and upon feeling the blunt cut, I pulled my hands away quickly. Molly noticed.

"Girl, don't worry none about your hair. It'll grow back," she told me.

I wasn't too sure about that. My cousin Josie's hair was shorter than anyone's hair I had ever seen, and it never grew. My aunt explained it to me by stating that Negroes' hair didn't grow, that the Lord had given Negro women other beauties to have . . .

"Lord give us brains," she'd said, thumping my head hard. "So you see, because you got all this hair, you must not got a brain in your head," she'd said and cackled.

Perhaps it was my aunt Rebecca I should thank for my intelligence, because I was driven to learn all I could. Unfortunately, book knowledge came easy. It was common sense I realized that I was lacking.

"Negroes' hair doesn't grow like that," I grumbled quickly. Molly seemed caught mid-thought as she gave me a close look.

"And what I give a damn about a Nigra's hair for?"

she asked me flatly. I said nothing in answer. She gave me a closer look, and then, suddenly, the room filled with a hearty belly laugh.

"Molly Duncan Holsted, if you ain't shootin' craps!" she blurted out before covering her mouth and staring at me again. I attempted to turn away, but she turned my face toward hers. "My God, I see it now," she remarked. "I ain't never been this close to many Nigras, mostly Mexicans where I'm from, but, shoot, I do see it now," she went on. "Take away them green eyes and all this straight hair and white skin, and we got a Nigra woman." She cackled. Her words made me flinch noticeably now.

"Molly . . . Miss Molly, I need to go," I said, starting for the screen door. She stopped me.

"Not so fast, you. Tell me first what you were running from back there in town," she said. "When I thought you were a white girl, I figured it was sumthin' serious. Now I'm just curious to know what it was."

The pain of my people's rejection had to show on my face, and I couldn't keep the tears from my eyes. The humiliation of Daryl's actions, too, broke my heart. The fact that he hadn't come after me had hit me hours earlier, as I drifted off to sleep in the car, but I had not wanted to think about it anymore, and so I'd blocked it out.

"I made a mistake," I said. My voice was shaky, and I was having a hard time thinking of a decent lie.

"Yeah, I've made a couple of those myself," Molly said, cackling like a hen.

"I really did come looking for my family. But I didn't find them," I told Molly over a big bowl of delicious hot soup. She was a wonderful cook, and while my palate was soothed, I told her all there was to tell, except for the forced sex that Daryl tried to have with me. I'm sure I made Betty Bickel into more a beast than she deserved, telling Molly that she had cut my hair for no good reason except that I had hair to cut and that she did not.

Molly shook her head, disgusted at how the colored people in that community had acted toward me.

"I say, forget 'em. Some people just like hurtin' others for no reason," Molly said, possibly still reflecting on her hatred for Brent Holsted. "It seems, to get along with folks, you have to hold a black wida in one hand and a diamondback in the other."

I looked at the time. It was late and I was tired. "Miss Molly, if I'm gonna find a place to land, I need to get started."

"Foolishness," Molly said upon my suggestion for her to drop me back off where she had found me.

"But, Miss Molly, I—"

"And it's just plain ol' Molly, please. You make me feel old with all that Miss stuff. Look, gal"—Molly then grabbed my arm and placed it next to her well-tanned one—"you're whiter'n me." She giggled.

"What does that mean?" I asked.

"It means, it's what's inside of you that matters . . . really. You may always have a colored heart, but that's between you and your God," she preached, wagging her finger in my face. "But on the outside, you're white . . . just like me. Now I don't know why the good Lord saw fit to give you a chance in life like this, or why we met up at a time like this in my life, but. . . ." She paused and thought in silence. "Why not use what you got to get somewhere in life? Why do you people always have to walk around with your heads down to the floor and feeling oppressed all the damn time? Shit! I'll show you some oppression . . . I'm oppressed!" She laughed, slapping the tender side of my arm hard. "Now, do you wanna work for me or not!" she asked.

"Well, I don't have anywheres else to—"

"Do you wanna work for me? Say hell yeah!" she yelped, sounding and looking even wilder about the eyes then she had earlier that afternoon.

"Well, I—"

"Say hell yeah, or I'm gonna drop you off, and, honey, you ain't got much more hair for that woman to cut off," she said.

"Hell yeah!" I yelped now, bursting into laughter.

Chapter 9

The state flag known as the Lone Star Flag was adopted in 1839. The red stands for bravery, the white represents purity, and the blue is for loyalty. The front of the state seal also has a lone star. The oak branch to the left of the star symbolizes strength, and the olive branch to the right of the star stands for peace. The reverse side of the seal includes a display of the six flags that have flown over Texas.

If I was gonna become a *native* Texan in the next four days, I thought I'd better get started learning a little about the state. Molly was pleased that I read so well and understood what I read even better.

Molly had decided not to drive. My first ride in a taxicab let us off at the train station. Molly explained to me that when we got to Texas, she would be putting me to work serving customers coffee and breakfast at her diner. I was barely listening to her as we boarded the train—the main car.

A ride in a cab and now getting a cabin car of a train, well, I might as well just say that my heart began to pound as I felt all eyes on me. Would I be thrown off this train the first time someone peeked in our room and spied me there? Would I be lynched this morning?

I had dreamed of this scene many times—me alone with white people, all tearing at me, trying to pull my skin from my body, the way a person would strip what was theirs away from a thief. I often dreamed that my skin didn't really belong to me, that somehow I had stolen it and that one day the true owner would come back for it.

When I'd left with Mrs. Griffith, I'd felt different. Maybe it was because I was a child and I knew, I knew who I was. I was black. But now I didn't have any idea.

"You having some problems, Emma?" Molly asked me, noting my stiff posture when she attempted to show me a seat next to a young girl who looked about my age.

Molly had begun calling me Emma immediately. She said the name Emerald sounded like I was labeling myself as a thing instead of a person, and she was making a point of letting me know that the days of being labeled were over. We were heading west, and all things good were about to happen . . . or so she promised.

I didn't know where this woman came from, or whether she was evil or good, or why she would want me to live with her. I was sick to my stomach every time I thought of the possible evils she could be hiding from me behind her pale blue eyes and carefree laughter, but I had no other choices at the time— or so I felt.

"No, ma'am," I said under my breath, scared to look her straight in the eyes as Molly was suddenly very white to me.

"I know you're nervous, but there's no need to be afraid," she said in a low voice, no doubt seeing the fear in my eyes now. She tipped the porter and closed the door to our bed car.

I know Molly thought that I was just nervous about leaving St. Louis for another strange place; she had no way of knowing my true feelings. She had no way of knowing how awful life had turned out at the end of my last train ride.

"Well, just settle in then, because this ride is gonna be just short of forever. I swear, next time I'm getting on an airplane." She pondered her statement. "Yes, the next time I travel, I'ma be somebody important."

The next day of our trip, Brent Holsted joined up with us. We met him for dinner. He had dressed in a suit, and Molly and I had dressed in what I called our Sunday best. Molly's entire countenance changed when he joined us at our table in the dining car. He was a handsome man who looked not much older than Molly. When he entered the car, looking all dapper and smooth, I could tell by the way she gripped my arm that at that moment she wanted me to stay quiet. I did.

Molly had slowly filled me in on many things about herself, and so far, nothing she had told me cleared up who she was or what she wanted from me. It had taken me a minute or two to realize that Molly was much younger than the now-deceased Mr. Holsted. True, she had told me that, but now seeing Mr. Holsted's son, Bret, it all came together in my head.

Many in the car were dressed nicely and appeared wealthy and refined. Molly was definitely in a class above the Griffiths. Mrs. Griffith had brought our food, homemade breads and jams. We'd eaten in our seats and had only been served beverages. This dinner with Molly and Bret was first class, I could tell, and I was scared witless.

After our meal, the colored waiter serving me

smiled and immediately poured me a cup of coffee and sat before me a large glob of ice cream sitting on a piece of pie. I just stared at him grinning at me, nodding and serving me—me, Emerald. I looked at the cup for a long time before Molly pushed it closer. "Drink up," she said.

"How much more food is coming?" I whispered, leaning close to her ear.

She grinned, clearing her throat, whispering back, "Honey, as much as they bring," and then letting out a belly laugh, bigger than one would think possible from such a small woman, "Silly girl," she added, fanning her gloved hand, putting on airs. Brent just smirked and rolled his eyes. Surely, he saw me as foolish and ill-mannered.

"You'd think these colleges would teach these kids manners," he said, fanning the waiter, who nodded and bowed quickly before spinning on his heels and heading toward the kitchen.

"But then what does a pretty girl like my niece here need with college, anyway?" Molly said, wrinkling up her nose flirtatiously.

I didn't know what she meant by that, and suddenly, this woman, who over the last few days had shown me a true fighting spirit, had turned into something out of a science fiction comic book. Surely, a mad scientist had taken her brain during the night. She was giggly and flirtatious and, well, just downright *girlie*.

When I glanced at Brent Holsted, who surprisingly found the comment humorous, my head spun with confusion. Taking a sip of the rich, flavorful coffee before me, I had to wonder, who were these people sitting in this booth with me?

Just then, Molly pushed the sugar closer to me. "Black coffee is a man's drink," she said now, giving a quick lesson in femininity. "I do see that college took the girl out of you, Emma." She giggled again.

Of course, I caught my tongue before reminding her of the hair-raising cup of black coffee she'd had the porter bring to us just that morning in our cabin. I'd swear to the fact that she'd added alcohol to it, because my head had spun all morning. But I said nothing. Apparently, Brent Holsted's presence had changed things. Somewhere between leaving St. Louis and meeting him, I had gone from a hired hand to her niece on a sabbatical from college. It was all somewhat confusing.

The next day, when we stepped off the train in Dallas, I breathed in the different air. I could tell I was a long way from home. I could feel the difference. My eyes burned as I fought back the tears of instantaneous loneliness. I missed my cousin Josie. I missed my aunt, my mother.

Again, I missed Noah.

Chapter 10

"We'll open right after we eat breakfast," Molly said, pulling off the frilly hat and turning to the grill. She then pointed to the number four on the menu. I would never forget that combination. It was Molly's best meal deal. I had it for breakfast every day for many months to come.

Molly had me stay in the back of the diner the first night we arrived. She was the owner of the diner and had converted the place out of what was once her original home, the one she lived in before marrying Buck Holsted. She had left one of the house's bedrooms attached to the back. After marrying the cattleman, she'd moved into the ranch house, which sat at the edge of town.

Buck Holsted had several homes, one being where Molly had cared for me the day we ran into each other in St. Louis. That was the one Brent had laid immediate claim to, as he had been raised in that house. But it was the ranch house Molly was most fond of and was planning to fight tooth and nail to keep.

"After I married Buck, I just stayed there in the big house and left this room as is," she said, turning on the light after we finally had ditched Brent Holsted and made our way by cab to the diner. I had wondered where Mr. Holsted was staying but didn't ask.

The room was quaint and clean. The bed was large and covered with heavy blankets. The furnishings were oak, and on the dresser sat a porcelain washbasin. Little did Molly know, this room was the best room I had ever stayed in. It was so private and comfortable and grown up.

But after dark hit that diner, I was scared out of my socks and spent a good portion of the night on my knees, asking God what was happening to me and why I was always ending up in a jam like this. And I prayed, respectfully, for a prompt answer, too—*if he didn't mind.*

I worked every day for nearly a week, from sunup until sundown. I was the hardest worker she had ever seen—next to herself, of course.

"That's what Buck always said about me," Molly said. "He said I was nearly as strong as him. But when you're the only girl in a house fulla boys, ya gotta be tough . . . or be gone." She laughed. "Buck always liked me for who I was"—she paused, sounding sad now—"I'm gonna miss that old man." She sighed, before hitting my arm and pointing at an apron. "Let's get this joint jumping, li'l girl," she then said, grinning wide and sliding a nickel in the jukebox. Bill Haley poured out. She began to do the jitterbug, urging me to join her. I wasn't much of a dancer and so declined, hopping up on a bar stool to watch.

The Molly I had met in St. Louis had returned full force. I had missed her. That other woman who rode the train and fawned over Brent Holsted—whoever she was—had wrecked my nerves to no end.

All week I watched Molly dealing with cowboys coming in the diner, truckers, loudmouths, and big families; she dealt with them all differently, yet professionally. Finally, I realized that she, in fact, had run that diner alone until hiring me.

"You're my first employee," she admitted, sliding up on the bar stool next to me, reaching under the counter glass and taking out a donut. She took a big bite.

"Doncha got no children?" I asked. She frowned.

"Don't I have any children?" she corrected me again. She had been doing that all week. Some rules of grammar I just didn't care to remember. "None I gave birth to. I have just the one stepson, Brent," she said, throwing out a hand gesture as if introducing him, even though he wasn't there. "God, has he become a pain in my derriere, and I don't know how much longer I can do this," Molly said, with a tight brow.

"Do what?" I asked innocently, heading to the icebox to make myself a float. One of the perks of working in the diner was that I got to have as many ice cream floats as I wanted.

"The fool thinks now that he has some rights to this diner . . . as if it wasn't my diner long before I married his father. Hogwash," she said, spitting out the words and then tossing back her thick curls. "Sure, Bucky did put a little money into this place, but it's mine. I'd fight the Devil to prove that!" she snapped, tossing the donut onto a saucer and jumping off the stool.

"I'm sorry," I said.

"Ohhh, don't be. You don't know anything about matters of finance . . . or men," she said flatly, as if either subject was something I would never be able to comprehend. "I just think me and Brent are too close in age for me to get his respect the normal way." She chuckled wickedly. "So I guess I have to try something else." She adjusted her belt and shook her leg, resembling an old television cowboy, like the ones I'd been watching on her television. That was another way Molly had the Griffiths beat: she had a television set, which I could watch without restrictions. What a new world I had open to me now.

"I'm only thirty, and he's thirty-two," she admitted now, telling me her age for the first time.

"I'm seventeen, almost eighteen," I admitted freely, slurping on my straw. That revelation snapped Molly to attention.

"Seventeen?" she gasped and then sighed, with a smile. "And such a pretty seventeen, too. I swear, I would never be able to guess that you're colored," she said, examining me closely again. "You told me about your mama, but you ain't said much about your pa."

"My pa?" I asked, caught off guard.

I had never been asked that before. Mostly everyone in my hometown already knew the answer to that question—some acting as if they knew even more than my mother or me.

"My pa"—I cleared my throat—"uh, he's dead?" I lied—maybe.

"You act like you don't know," she said, winking with her words, as was her manner. She was a snappy lady, and I liked the way she would do that—winking and blowing kisses to certain customers when they would leave. It was classy—she was very classy—in my humble opinion. I wanted to be like her.

"Well, I don't, really," I admitted. Molly stood and wiped her hands on the towel lying over the counter, as if the conversation was on the verge of becoming uncomfortable.

"Well, no loss. I don't know my daddy, neither," she said quickly, and to my surprise. She then took the plates off the counter, left from the last of the dinner crowd. "My mama told me that he was just plain-o waste of time and nowhere needed around our house." Molly was sounding strong and independent. "But it's something we, as *proper ladies,* never talk about. You understand?" she said, sounding as though another lesson in living was about to start. I nodded. Instead of getting any deeper into the conversation, however, Molly slipped a few more nickels in the jukebox and held out her hands for me to join her.

"I can't dance," I informed her.

"What? I can't believe a Negro that can't dance. I'll be dipped. Come on now. We gotta get you on the dance floor. How are we supposed to get you married up if you can't dance? I just added in a bunch of new music from that new guy Bill Haley. I just love that 'Shake, Rattle and Roll.' Oohh wee. It gets me movin'," she said, wriggling her hips and snapping her fingers. "Now come on and just follow my lead."

"Husband! I thought you said—"

"I said my daddy wasn't worth nothing. We gonna get you a man worth a million dollars, if I'm lucky."

I didn't have the heart to tell her I was already married. She seemed convinced that I was wife material. I took her hands, trying to follow her quick-moving steps. Finally, she shook her head. "I can't believe it. Well, you gonna have to come out to the ranch and get Manuela and Jessie to teach you a thing or two. For now, let's get back to these dishes."

"Why haven't you ever hired anybody to do some of these dishes, Molly?" I asked, allowing a groan to quickly chase my words. She tied on a white apron, replacing the red one she wore to serve. I, too, replaced my red one with a white one.

"I just did," she laughed, pointing at me. "Actually, I couldn't afford anybody except maybe some Mexican or colored boy. And, frankly, I don't have time for their lazy asses," she said, without flinching.

Of course, I couldn't do the same.

"What's wrong with you?" she asked, noticing my tight lips and wide eyes.

"Nothing," I said, keeping silent now. I quickly started working on the dishes. I felt the need to do my best tonight. I would never want her to use such a despicable tone about me.

"Oh yeah, I guess I should be thinking about paying you something for working here," she said, joining me at the big sink after making sure all the tables were wiped down.

"No, the room is plenty," I told her, answering her quickly so that she wouldn't have time to think of anything else to say.

"Now, girl, you need to have some money in your pocket. And besides, you can't just stay in that room forever. You'll never get ahead taking the least that people offer you. Think big!" she said, using her hands, spread wide above her head, to show me just how big to think. "You're a pretty girl. You need to think big," she said, again implying a connection between my looks and where I could get in life. A moment later she must have realized her earlier comment hurt my feelings.

"And that thing I said about the lazy asses them boys have. Well, I meant it! And if you want a man who is worth you, then you have to be worth more to yourself."

I stayed a month longer in that room before Molly invited me to the big house. It was bigger than I'd imagined. It was truly a ranch, spread out. The house was at least half of the one hundred acres of land it sat on—at least it looked as such, anyway.

Molly had horses and cows, along with a lot of

ranch help—a Mexican family named Garcia. The father's name was Jesus; the mother's, Maria; and the six children all were named after Catholic saints that I'd heard of. I had never seen many Mexicans before, but I found out quickly that they were just another race that was looked down on for being who they were, and they had grown to accept the treatment. They cooked really good and loved to dance, especially their two older children, Antony and Manuela, who quickly became friends with me, being my age. Antony was a year older, and Manuela, just a few months younger.

Papa Jesus and I had many heated discussions about the unfair life of ethnic races, war, politics, and other grown-up issues. He was always amazed at how someone like me could show so much compassion for the underdogs, considering what a blessed life I had—as a young, privileged white girl. I would simply smile and nod, keeping my promise to Molly to never reveal the truth about my race to anyone. But it seemed as if Papa Jesus noticed something odd about me, because of how passionate I was about the rights of colored people.

By the way, I was speaking Spanish fluently within three months.

Chapter 11

Summer of 1954

Summer came in hot, and for the first time, I was somewhat happy about my shorter hair. It was growing back slowly but still had not reached my shoulders. But with the sweltering heat melting Holsted Ranch, I was glad to wear it short and cool. Molly, in a crazy mood, had convinced me to dye my black hair blond to match hers. Forgetting about my ethnicity, we ended up with red instead, but that was fine. She said red was just as much fun. Truly, she had become like a sister to me.

"Just never tell anyone you're Negro," Molly said, swearing me to secrecy.

I will never forget my driving lessons, cookouts out on the range, dancing at the cowboy bars, where she would slip me in the back door because she knew the owner. I learned to smoke, drink, and cuss like a real Texan. I learned it all, short of spitting tobacco, as Molly said, "That ain't ladylike." But speaking of being a lady, Molly wasn't short on charm, and she gave me many lessons on being a gracious hostess, even when I didn't care for my visitors. She had to entertain many of Buck's lingering friends, old-timers who bored Molly senseless, yet together we kept them coming, and their dollars of contributions, to keep the ranch running in Buck's memory.

I hardly ever thought about Peachy anymore, and Noah filled only my dreams now as I was sure I would never see his face again. The hardest part of all of this was to believe that Molly truly had no ulterior motives or plans for me and that all she really wanted was for me to work for her in her diner and be her friend.

Needless to say, I thanked God every night for the Bickels and their meanness, for if it hadn't been for them, I might not have run into Molly Duncan Holsted. I must admit, I did think about Daryl from time to time, but that was only because of how close he came to getting where only Noah had been. It had nothing to do with love, so the memory didn't count really.

Antony and Manuela were my best friends, even though we really didn't do much together outside the ranch. It was bad enough folks mumbled behind me and Molly's back whenever we went into town together, but I didn't want to hear anything they might have to say about Antony and Manuela.

I heard the bad-mouthers. They said Molly was a social climber and a gold digger. I had never heard the terms before, but they didn't sound very nice. Molly worked hard to keep things running at that ranch, and they had no call to bad-mouth her that way. However, I held my tongue as it was no telling what they said about me.

Life couldn't have been easier there on Molly's ranch. She seemed happy and carefree, and, therefore, I felt the same way. I'd not given another thought to the possibilities of her ever losing the ranch to Brent, or anyone else, for that matter. I just spent my time pumping nickels into the jukebox at the diner and swinging my hips to Bill Haley and his Comets. Perhaps that's why she never talked business with me or revealed the details of her and Brent's secret weekend meetings. She would simply leave some Fridays and return on Sunday—often flustered and upset.

Business at the diner was constant. Molly paid me movie money, which I usually just squirreled away for a rainy day or gave to Mrs. Garcia for her help. While Molly was gone, I had full run of the diner, and unbeknownst to her, I had hired on Mrs. Garcia to help me in the kitchen. Therefore, I had a little extra time to wander around in town, window-shopping.

Time had passed like minutes for us, and the year flew by like a week. It was the Fourth of July, and downtown there was a festival—Texas style, with music and free barbeque—celebrating rumors that the war was coming to an end. Earlier in the day, church bazaars piggybacked on the event, setting up their tables in the park, along with pies and cakes for sale. But they, too, were winding down as a night of spectacular fireworks displays had already begun to fill the sky. Missing the churchy part as well as the "let's hear it for the boys" part of the day was fine by me; I wasn't in the mood for war propaganda or fake church people, who smiled in your face yet talked badly about you behind your back. Molly wasn't a churchgoer and so was quite the subject of gossip in that town. I was just glad they weren't talking about me—at least not within earshot. Living with Molly had kept me out of the limelight for quite a while now; she was such an independent woman, very much ahead of her time. She wasn't shy, to say the least, and her efforts to *catch a man* were becoming renowned. I didn't fault her for enjoying the company of menfolks. She was a pretty woman and young at heart. Deep inside, I half hoped she and Brent would hit it off one day, but I had no real hopes of that. She assured me Brent was the bane of her existence.

I wasn't thinking about none of that stuff tonight, though. The only rumor interesting me was the one that maybe that new singer that was taking the South by storm would show up at this festival—Elvis Presley. He was my only thought tonight. I dressed in a cool eyelet summer dress, shaved my legs, and slipped into some flats. Molly had insisted I add a touch of red to my lips to accentuate my eyes, and so I did. I pulled into town and parked near the soda fountain. Bob Drysdale smiled at me through the window while closing his barbershop for the night as I sauntered toward the bright lights of the festival. He'd been to the ranch for dinner once, but Molly said something about him being slim pickins, and he was never invited back. He didn't seem her type, anyway, and he sure wasn't mine, if that crazy thought had crossed her mind.

I saw many of the families and couples with food baskets and blankets, as if they had planned to lounge the evening away, but not me. I didn't need all that, as I intended to be on my feet, having grown nearly addicted to the rock and roll music I heard on the radio. If I had to go a day without hearing it, I thought I would just die. So finding out there was to be live music here at this festival, I just had to come. Even if I had to dance alone, I was gonna cut a rug before this night was over. Swinging my purse, carefree-like, I nearly skipped to the park.

"Hey there, pretty girl," I heard someone call to me from alongside the malt shop.

It was Scott Baker. He was a rebel who rode a motorcycle. I knew he liked me, but according to Molly, he wasn't my type. He was a greaser and a hood. Molly had told me he was trouble a long time ago. And Molly had been good to me, so I listened. Dreamboat or not, Scott Baker was off-limits!

"I'm not listening to you, Scott Baker," I said smartly as I quickly passed him by. He rushed out to the street to catch up with me.

"So you dig rock 'n' roll, huh?" he asked me tauntingly.

I stopped walking for a second to roll my eyes hard. They landed on his blue ones, with flakes of grey floating through. He was dreamy and he knew it. Much of his hard exterior was just an act, as I'd heard he'd dropped out of school to help his father drive a truck for a moving company, to support his siblings after his mother abandoned the family. That was one of the main reasons he didn't go to war. He was needed at home. Let him tell it, he was a big-time desperado . . . a conscientious objector . . . et cetera.

"I figured you for a square. Didn't think you were hip to all this jive," he said. "I'd never thought I'd see you out on a Saturday night, either, with your own wheels, I might add." It had gotten around quickly that I had a new car. Of course, no one was the wiser as to how much begging it took to get it. I had promised Molly a lifetime of servitude in order for her to cosign.

"Look, Scott, I'm not going to talk to you. I'm here to see the band," I insisted weakly before moving on toward the entrance gate, with a little extra swing in my hips. I knew it would wig him out seeing me flirt like that. I also knew it would wig out Molly if she saw me talking to him, but I was older now and thought it time I showed my age. I was a young woman now and had worked hard to get where I was—a good life, no troubles.

Sure, it was a fake life based entirely on lies and fraud, but I had made it work and I was happy.

"We gonna dance together tonight, Emma. You and me, nice and slow," Scott whispered in my ear, still keeping up with my quick strides. He was a lot taller than I was, and so I felt like he was huddled over me like a vulture. I really didn't like Scott much; I just enjoyed looking at him—from a distance. He was truly starting to annoy me.

Just then, a marine in full uniform appeared from the crowd. He looked intimidating and official. The rumors of war ending were everywhere, but still the troops had yet to come home. I just had to figure that maybe there were some troops getting a little leave time while the government decided if they would really free them or start another war. As hot as it was, the marine wasn't even sweating, but I figured he had to be sweltering in that uniform. I saw Scott's eyes widen.

"This man bothering you, miss?" the Marine asked, with his hands folded behind his back and his chiseled chin stiff. I looked around, wondering if perhaps there was to be a police action over Scott's little pestering, and although he did bug me, I didn't want him to go to jail over it.

"No, no," I stammered.

"Beat it," the officer said to Scott now, with his voice deep and rumbling.

"You can't tell me—," Scott began.

"Look, Scott, do what he says," I quickly admonished. I was nervous enough for the both of us, never being one for arguing with officials.

Cursing and spitting, Scott kicked the dirt and

strolled off, trying hard to hold on to his cool. He was angry and I could tell.

I thanked the officer and ran in the direction Scott had gone. Now the shoe was on the other foot as I ran behind his quick steps like a puppy. "Look, Scott, I didn't cause that. Maybe if you didn't act and look like such a bad actor, the cops wouldn't bug you so much."

"What do you know about it . . . or me?" he growled.

"I know you need better friends. You need to stop hanging out on street corners," I started to fuss. I was going to sit him straight on some things. He stopped dead in his tracks.

"So, where do you say we hang out?" he then asked. I looked around as if he had spoken to someone behind me . . . the *someone* who had remotely suggested to him that we become friends. My mind quickly went to Molly and her words about men. The bad ones were for looking only . . . distance between you and them was your best bet. I felt myself step back.

"Yeah, that's what I thought, chicky," he said to me. He kissed me quickly on the lips, and then, clicking his teeth, he pulled out a cigarette and lit it. "You couldn't handle me, anyway." He smiled.

He was a true looker that Scott Baker, a dreamboat of major proportions. I felt a thickness form in my throat and gulped it down. I wanted to deny his words, but he was telling it straight. Scott was trouble with a capital *T*.

Maybe it was my silence, maybe it was the way I stared at him, but after a couple of drags from his cigarette, he reached out for my hand and I gave it to him, and together we headed for his motorcycle. There was nothing about Scott the boy I wanted, but there was something about Scott the rebel that spoke to me. I could relate to the pureness of his rebellion, the need for the freedom to be who he wanted to be whenever he wanted to be that.

I climbed on his motorcycle and slid close in, hugging his waist tight. He glanced over his shoulder at me and grinned. I was grinning so hard, my face ached. I couldn't help it. He put his foot on the gas pedal, revved up the engine, then pulled off. We rode for a long time, until we reached the outskirts of town, turning onto a long, narrow unpaved road. Soon we came upon a farmhouse, where he stopped the bike and I climbed off.

"You live here?" I asked.

"Yeah, me, my pop, and the kids."

"Kids? Where is your mother?"

"She took off a long time ago," he said, looking for a response. I tried hard not to show any emotion. But life without a mother was tough . . . I knew that much.

"Where are the children? Where is your dad?" I asked, following him toward the front door.

"They stay with my aunt while my pop is at work. He works out at the compress when we're not on the road. . . . Anyway, he won't be home until late." Scott opened the door.

The house was in sore need of a woman's touch. It was cluttered and disorganized, but I was surprised to find the kitchen clean and almost presentable.

"Want something to drink?"

"No, thanks," I said.

"Why not? I know your throat is dry."

"No, really, I'm fine. Actually, I kinda wanna get back to town."

"We just got here, chicky," he said, pulling me into an embrace. "Don't you wanna spend a little time with me? I hear you like to have fun."

"I'm not that kind of girl," I said, pushing free.

"Yeah, right. . . . You're Molly's kin. . . . You're that kind of girl." He laughed.

"What the hell does that mean?" I asked, knowing the answer.

"She's a chippy. My pop tells me she'll do anything for a dollar," he said. "And he should know. He ain't got no dollars and therefore . . ." He let the insinuation hang.

I slapped him without thinking twice, and he quickly returned the action. I grabbed at the sting and then turned to leave, but Scott grabbed my arm and pulled me back to him.

"Look, all I wanted was to show you a nice time tonight, but, no, you made it bad, Em, and for no good reason. You treat me like I'm a leper. Everybody does, and I'm sick of it."

"What?"

"You act like you're too good for me," he said.

"That's because I am," I smarted off. I hated my words but couldn't stop them. I sounded haughty and evil, but he had slapped me hard, and I was pretty mad. "Now take me back to town."

"Me?" He laughed. "You can get back to town on your own since you're so much better than me," he said, storming into the kitchen, swinging open the refrigerator, and pulling out a beer.

I looked around the living room for a telephone. Molly had one, but Scott and his father did not. So I found a place to sit instead.

"Fine. I'll wait for your dad to get home and tell him you kidnapped me then." I pouted.

He rolled his eyes, possibly thinking of the beating he would receive when his dad got home after a long night of working. He'd come home to find a young girl claiming Scott had kidnapped her and was planning evil things. I would be crying my eyes out and acting crazed. Yep, Scott was gonna get it.

"Get up. Let's go," he growled. I shook my head. "Get up!" he screamed, jerking me to my feet.

"Sheesh, what a bully," I told him. He must have thought I was flirting, because he kissed me again. I didn't fight him, but I didn't kiss him back.

"What a tease," he said before dragging me from the house and out to the motorcycle. The ride back home was not quite as exciting as the ride there.

Dropping me at my car, I quickly climbed in without looking at him. I started up the engine and drove off, without so much as a good night. My guilt was overwhelming. I had again come close to doing something bad with the wrong boy. Not since Daryl had I gotten this close to messing my life up. I knew Molly would never forgive me if I had done anything with Scott willingly. She had taught me so much about self-respect. Even knowing I was black hadn't stopped her from teaching me how to be successful in life. I was happy, more happy than I thought I would ever be. I finally was thinking that being white was going to work out. I could speak my mind, and people listened.

When I got home, I walked into the main house, and suddenly, from behind the large French doors leading to the smoking room, I heard an unfamiliar sound. The sound tightened my belly, giving me a sick feeling deep inside. The longer I stood there, the more the sound became recognizable, like that of two animals fighting. Grunting, squealing, snorting—yes, it sounded like pigs tussling over some slop. Then I began to hear human voices mixed in—deep and guttural sounding. Primal. It was Molly's voice and the one voice I'd heard many times, but for the life of me, I wanted to be mistaken this day.

"Now I really feel like my daddy, getting sex for a dollar," he chortled. I could hear moving around, and so I decided I'd better get outta there, but my feet didn't match the speed of my thoughts, and the doors opened before I could move. My eyes met Brent's face, reddened in a flush. He smiled and outstretched his hand.

"Hello there, Em," he said to me. Many people, not just Scott, had taken to shortening my name that way, and Brent acting formally with me was not so uncommon, either.

I looked at the hand, and thinking of the possible places it had just been, I opted not to shake it, smiling and nodding instead.

Molly hurried around in the parlor, straightening pillowing and fluffing cushions. She was as red as a beet herself.

"Emma, what are you doing here? I thought you were going to town to see Elvin Priestly or whoever?" Molly asked over her shoulder. I noticed the inside flap of her dress was out. The ruffled sight of her would have been almost humorous if the reasons weren't so tragic. I thought about what I had heard Scott say just tonight about Molly and what she would do for money. I didn't want to believe it, but she hadn't given me much choice.

I never wanted a man to touch me that way or have control over me the way she had apparently allowed her life to be controlled by Brent Holsted. Whether she knew it or not, she was now his slave, and I knew about slavery, as I, too, had, through my actions, sold my soul for what I hoped would be a better life. I had given up my race to supposedly find a better one. I, too, was a slave, and now she and I were equal. My heart hurt, and I was immediately confused.

Wanting to respect Molly a moment or two longer, I ran quickly to my room and locked the door behind me.

Rumors of war ending didn't mean our boys got to come home. No, not while the cold war still raged in front of the blinded eyes of Americans. I took it personally, another act of betrayal. I was taking everything to heart lately. I took everything as a personal affront to my life. My mother hadn't been straight with me about life, Greta Griffith had used me to enhance her wretched life, I felt like Noah had abandoned me and the life we could have had together, although I was the one who left town, and Molly had let me down, and therefore, what else could life hold for me? Nothing good . . . not from where I stood. And the lies of the government . . . did I dare address those? Little did the poor soldiers know that cold conflict would soon erupt and they would soon be put smack dab in the middle of the longest and most impressive war of that century—the Vietnam conflict.

However, Molly and I were in a war on a civilian level, alongside those worldwide confrontations.

That Christmas, as a peace offering, I bought Molly a cameo pin, which she seemed to cherish, wearing it every day. What she didn't know was that I also bought all of the Garcias a gift as well and ate dinner at their home Christmas Eve, when Molly thought I had gone to Mass. She just knew she had made me a Catholic, but there was nothing about praying to dead saints that had done something for me that made me want to believe in them.

Frankly, I didn't believe in many man-made religions, and it wasn't as if they had shown me much to make me feel differently. Life was what you made it. And, as of late, there had been no miracles shown to me. Getting on my knees did nothing but make them rough and sore. That was how I felt. My heart was hardened, calloused from having to heal without salve from the breakage that had taken place a long time prior.

It was days after the holiday when Brent Holsted visited unexpectedly and left Molly in foul humor. I was determined to get to the bottom of that man sooner or later. Their little tête-à-têtes had gone on for way too long. Today he left Molly near tears. She dashed into the house after walking with him to his car and up to her room, slamming the door and locking it.

I called to her, but she told me to go away and leave her alone. I didn't take her tone personally and was not offended. Nothing really offended me much anymore. I simply went out the back door, avoiding Brent's exit, to visit with Mrs. Garcia.

"Maria, what do you know about Mr. Holsted?" I asked her as together we made tortillas in her kitchen. She began speaking in quick, angry Spanish until I grabbed her arm. She must have thought I was Manuela the way she tore into the language as if I was born speaking it.

"English, Maria. Please, I can't follow you." I laughed. Although I understood Spanish, when Maria was in a tizzy, I couldn't interpret what she was saying. She then, with a scowl, told me a little about Mr. Holsted.

"He's a thief and a liar, and he's using Miss Molly . . . like a . . ." She groped for words until finally one came. "Chippy," she spat.

"Chippy? What is that?" I asked, having heard it several times over the last few months. Just the sound of it caused me to chuckle, especially not knowing exactly what it meant.

"*Maria, silencio!*" Papa Garcia snapped, silencing his wife immediately upon entering the house and hearing her talking with me about Brent Holsted.

Maria wiped her hands on her apron and went over to the stove, turning the blaze on high, no doubt as high as her anger had gotten at just the thought of the situation between Molly and Brent. I looked at

Papa Garcia and then back at Maria, hoping there were no hurt feelings developing.

Manuela was engaged to be married, and so spending time with her was no longer an option, and Antony was very shy and so, without Manuela as a cover for his feelings, he often avoided me like the plague. So I just went back to the house to wait for Molly to come from her room. It took over an hour, but finally she did. By then I was watching television. She had finally purchased a color TV, and I was hooked. I was easily addicted to things like the radio and television. Perhaps it was my age or my boredom, but I enjoyed being informed as well as entertained. Television opened the doors of propaganda wider than I'd ever imagined they could be, and commercials were my favorite pastime.

"We need to talk, sugar," Molly said to me after a couple more good sniffs. Reluctantly, I pulled away from the boob tube.

"Uh-huh," I hummed.

"We got trouble," she said.

"Trouble?" She had my attention now.

"Seems as my plans for survival haven't panned out as well as I had expected. I had hopes that life here on this ranch would get easier with the . . . umm"—she paused—"investors that have shown interest. . . ." She stumbled over her words. My memory flashed back to the day Brent had been in the parlor, and I wondered now about how many *investors* might have shown their *interest* right under my nose.

"I see. I wasn't aware we were having financial problems," I said, trying to sound older than my years. I'd been acting older for so long, I really didn't know how old I was anymore.

"So, I'm gonna need your help. Remember when you came, I told you that one day you would have to save my life just like I had saved yours?" she asked. Actually, I never remember her saying anything so drastic, but I nodded. I felt awful for her; who knows how long she'd been giving herself to Brent Holsted in trade for her home. "Good. Because it looks like I'm gonna have to call in that favor."

"Pardon? What kind of favor would that be?"

"Look, you're old enough to start understanding some things, and, well, you need to understand the relationship between me and Brent. Well, the relationship there used to be between Brent and me. Looks like he's about to get married and, well . . ." She pushed her thick blond mane out of her face and sighed heavily. "Well, things around here are gonna change unless I can produce some money . . . and fast. I don't have a clue who can help me. I've gone through about everybody." She flopped onto the sofa.

I think she meant to mumble the part about going through nearly everyone. I thought back to Maria's words earlier that afternoon. "Molly, you're not a chippy," I said, sitting down by her. She raised her head, pulling her hair out of her face.

"What did you say?" she asked me, her words swelling with anger. I moved back.

"Nothing," I said, reneging on my words.

"Who called me that?" she asked, growing more agitated.

"Nobody," I lied. There was no way I was going to tell her Maria said it, nor was I gonna mention Scott's name in the house. She'd have blown a gasket, thinking I'd been talking to the likes of him. It wasn't as if he hadn't come by the diner nearly every day on his way home. Supposedly, he'd gotten a job or whatever. I made sure I never waited on him.

"Who ever said that is a damned . . ." She stifled her words. "I've worked hard my whole life. I deserve the life I have here, and I'da done whatever it took to keep it. Do you understand me?" she yelled, jumping to her feet. "If I had to sleep with Brent Holsted to keep this place, then so be it. If you had to sleep with Brent Holsted, you would have," she added, causing my stomach to turn slightly.

"I wouldn't do anything like that. I won't!" I screamed, unable to believe she was saying such horrible things. What was going through her head?

Perhaps it was because Manuela was about to be married off now that she thought I was anywhere near old enough to hear and understand what she was implying. I was in denial when it came to the reasons behind her introducing me to older men, men her age. I was big on politics but light on math, but suddenly, it was all adding up, and I didn't like the sum of it all. I had a bad feeling that with things headed way south between her and Brent, I was about to be her next meal ticket. All I could think about was the reality of the whole thing: Molly marrying me off to the first old white man that asked. It was reminiscent of a time I never wanted to live through. Heck, just living during the residual of it was hard enough. Of course, whoever the stool pigeon was about to be, he would be completely unaware of my race, but I wasn't.

"Well, Missy, you're gonna do somethin'. Life ain't a free ride."

"Molly, this ain't right, you asking me to do this."

"You don't even know what I'm asking you to do. Hell, it ain't like I'm really asking you to sleep with that knucklehead Brent. I wouldn't do that to ya, honey. Look, I was just mad. I know what folks think about me and what they're sayin', and I'm sorry if it is causing you trouble, but just think about the trouble you would have had in life had anybody known the truth about you."

"Molly—," I started, only to have her shush me.

"I'm not threatening you. I'm just reminding you. Think about what your mother wanted for you . . . a better life. Well, honey, you can't say you haven't had one with me, right?"

I nodded. "Yes."

"Well, I'm just saying that now you have to do what you have to do to keep it that way. You have to solidify your life . . . our life. You're not just some little Negra refugee. You're a full-fledged white woman, and as such, we have certain responsibilities in society, and, hell, being homeless ain't one of them."

"What do you want me to do?" I asked.

"I want you to help me. I want you to use what God and your daddy gave you to help me," Molly said, fighting back more tears.

What was I thinking? I loved Molly, but I wasn't gonna do this. I wasn't going to do what she had done for money. Was I?

Who cared that I changed my race for a better life. I wasn't going to give up my body for one! And how dare she ask me to.

"I'll do it, but I don't have to like it," I said, my voice barely leaving my throat. Molly cried harder now, reality, no doubt, hitting her hard—the reality of what our relationship was becoming, and what it had become.

It was obvious that Molly knew nothing about parenting. It was even more clear that both of us were simply two women bumbling around in a man's world.

Life was changing, in just a year, month, day, moment. The life of Emerald Jackson was changing again, taking her further and further from the life she had had that summer she was stopped from being colored.

Chapter 12

New Year's was upon us. Molly closed the diner that day as she was going to have a large spread at the big house. Since our conversation, Molly had had many friends come to the house on the weekends. She had become quite the socialite in just this last few weeks. One of her male friends—he was at least forty, pale white, and smelled of chewing tobacco and leather—had expressed interest in me on one of his visits, but Molly quickly nipped it in the bud, even before I did. I think it was my quick tongue that had her on her toes. I had become quite a firecracker and wasn't very friendly. I had agreed to be sold off, but at least she was willing to work with me a little, meaning, if he flat out disgusted me, I didn't have to let it go any further, and so far, all of the men who had visited made me sick.

Molly didn't realize how much I had begun to dream about my Noah, how my nights were filled with him, how my nose filled with his scent up to the rising of the sun, how my dreams filled with his black beauty. Maybe it was that I was a woman now, and my heart had finally grown up and made up its mind on who to allow in. I was no longer the fickle teenager whose head turned at every chance for a cute face or broad shoulder.

All I could hope for was that somewhere in God's heart, he could forgive me for my actions of the last few years and grant me this one blessing: to wake up, with my life to this point just a dream. How I wanted to wake up at my mother's side. But instead, this morning I woke up in my big feather bed to the sounds of the delivery truck outside bringing in extra supplies for Molly's fancy party.

Before the guests arrived that evening, Molly had spent a long time dressing upstairs. After a quick bath, I was ready in fifteen minutes for this shindig, as it just wasn't going to be a big deal to me. I had put on a pair of my favorite jeans and snakeskin boots, pulled my dark-rooted hair into a ponytail, and called it done. Noting Molly's delay in coming down, I slipped into the kitchen. I sure didn't want to entertain any early birds.

Since Mrs. Garcia's preparations for Manuela's wedding were keeping her busy, for this soiree, Molly had hired help to cook, a couple of black women, who spent the entire day in the kitchen. Molly, despite our money issues, still had champagne taste, and so hired help was not a second thought to her, even though I wasn't sure when the last time was that the Garcias had seen a dime from Molly's purse.

I felt an urge to go into the kitchen and talk with the two women there. I craved their company, and for the first time in weeks, I wanted to eat what was being cooked. The scented pots reminded me of my home and my community. Although I had often been met with rejection and meanness while growing up, I knew where my roots lay. I knew my culture—rich and full of music and beauty and good food. I missed it. I missed my home, my life . . . Noah. I'd had my fill of these cowboys and this dust bowl. I was ready to go home.

Mary and Lisabeth, the women in the kitchen, noticed me but said nothing as I milled around the large tiled kitchen, looking in pots and taking in the rich aromas. I could tell they wanted to tell me to get. I could see it on the tips of their tongues—just like the women back home. They hated "chirrins" in the kitchen, meddlin'.

"Is it almost done?" I finally asked Lisabeth, who glared at me just a little bit.

"Naw," she snapped, with a quick scowl.

"You making white gravy? Where is the brown gravy? Did you make sure there was some hot sauce around? What? No collards?" I asked, looking over the meal. She eyed me now, from head to toe.

"What choo know about collards?" she asked me, receiving a hard elbow from Mary, who seemed to think that I might be egging on a confrontation. I thought perhaps Mary worried that I would fire Lisabeth for talking back to me. I wanted to let her know that there'd be no firing done today, and if she wanted to fight me for just asking a simple question, I welcomed the fight. I needed it. Fighting, too, reminded me of home.

"I know lots about collards," I said, sounding like a braggart, "but then again, my aunt Rebecca James useta cook up the best messa greens in Shreveport. My mama had said it was her cooking that got her married off so many times."

Lisabeth sucked her teeth in growing irritation. "You need to go get dressed for dinner so you can meet Miss Molly's guest that's starting to come in," Lisabeth instructed, looking at my jeans.

"I am dressed," I smarted off, noticing Lisabeth's

expression changing to one fit to be tied. I could tell she wanted to snatch me out of my socks for smarting off to her this way. I could tell she had children, probably my age, who wouldn't have dared to talk back to her this way. My stomach tightened as she glared at me. I almost wanted to brace myself against the blow I was sure to receive. However, there was nothing. My tightly shut eyes opened to find only Mary looking at me. She had curiosity on her face. It looked as if she wondered why I was afraid of Lisabeth, who had gone out of the kitchen to serve hors d'oeuvres to the early guest. I cleared my throat and smoothed down my blouse, embarrassed just a little.

"What part of Shreveport you from?" Mary asked me. Feeling my game coming back to haunt me now, I shrugged stupidly. "Cuz the only Rebecca James I know of is a colored woman," she said.

"You know my aunt Rebecca?" I exclaimed before realizing what our exchange meant. Silence covered us.

"You're Em'rald, aren't you?" Mary asked me now. I was sure she saw my legs buckle, as I felt weak with the sound of my own name being said with the accent that felt natural on it. It had been a long time since I'd heard it with so much inflection.

"Yes . . . yes, I am. How do you know of me?" I gasped, with glee. Mary smiled at me with somewhat of a crooked smile and continued stirring the cake mix as if the answer did nothing but amuse her slightly.

"Tell me how you know," I said. I got only silence now. "Mary . . . tell me! And are you from my hometown? Do you know my people? Tell what you know from home," I said again, and again, she seemed to ignore me, pouring the mix in the pan.

I grew instantly furious, and grabbing the bowl from

her hands, I flung it as hard as I could, sending it smashing against the far wall. Mary glared at me, and then, like a cat, she jumped at me, tearing my blouse. My mind spun for only second. Then a rage from an unknown source came up in me, and I tore into her. On the floor we tumbled, kicking and scratching at each other. She cursed me and vice versa as both of us aimed hatred and anger at each other that neither of us deserved.

At that moment, Molly rushed into the kitchen, with the smelly man who liked me moving in front of her.

"What goes on here?" he called out. Molly pushed past him.

"Please, Herbert, I can handle this," Molly insisted. Lisabeth had hurried back into the kitchen and had pulled us apart. Both of us stood, soiled, heated, and breathing heavily, with anger still flaring our nostrils.

Molly's low-cut black dress, covered with silver, glittery sequins, had her looking like a starlet, and I felt bad immediately for how I had spoiled things. Her hair was high on her head, and her face was painted unlike I had ever seen before. She was beautiful. I could see how she had landed a millionaire oilman like Bucky Holsted. She, no doubt, had her sights on one of the millionaires there that night. Maybe I wouldn't have to marry after all. Maybe Molly was going to take care of things on her own, and I was ruining things. I ran from the kitchen in tears.

Unbelievably, Molly, somehow with the grace of a queen, saved the evening. With Texas charm, she turned the entire kitchen fiasco into a laughing matter within minutes. I could hear them from my room. I thought about Mary and hoped that my actions hadn't cost her a job, but I was far too ashamed to come out and speak to her or defend her. But I knew I would have to make this night up to everyone, somehow.

A quick bath and a change of clothes, I felt, would be a good start. I even put on a little make-up to cover the light bruising that Mary's slug had caused.

"What a stupid girl," I said about Mary under my breath as I felt my composure returning. "What an evil, stupid girl. All she had to do was tell me about . . ." I stopped my words and thoughts, feeling my anger returning a little. Couldn't she see how much I needed to hear news from home? This girl knew me, which meant she knew about me and what I had done. All I could figure was that she was angry.

When I came down the stairs, all the gentlemen stood, greeting me with Stetsons in hand. "To the next Rocky Marciano," the smelly man announced, causing the room to burst into laughter. I felt instantly flushed with embarrassment. I looked around for Molly, who winked at me. For some reason, she seemed almost pleased with me, as if my rough and rugged actions in the kitchen made her proud somehow.

Mary had gone home, and Lisabeth had called over a friend to take her place serving the meal. Needless to say, I was unable to make eye contact with Lisabeth. My shame was great, and I knew I would be finding out where they lived and paying them a visit as soon as I could.

After the meal, Molly led her adult guests into the parlor for conversation, smokes, and cognac. She didn't hesitate to hint that I was not invited, by instructing all to bid me good night before she and they disappeared behind the large French doors.

"Feelin' kinda left out, eh?" I heard from behind me, suddenly, as I stood staring at the doors closing in my face. I turned quickly to find Denny Johnson. He was older than I was, but apparently, even being twenty hadn't helped tonight. He was still too young to get into the parlor.

"I started to leave, but I figured, what the hell, they'll all be so sloshed in a little while, I might even get a beer," he said and laughed. He was cute, and though what he said wasn't funny, the dimple that came to his cheek helped in getting a giggle out of me.

"So that girl you walloped in the kitchen, what was her name?" he asked. Puddentane came to my mind and out of my mouth before anything else. He laughed at me.

"Puddentane," he repeated, this Texas drawl coming out all over me. "So you fight for a living, or is this just a new hobby?" he teased, chuckling at his own joke.

"Please stop," I begged. Feeling shame, I covered my face. He pulled my hand down.

"Don't. A face that pretty should never be covered." He flirted now. "Let's talk awhile, Em," he offered, sitting back comfortably on the sofa. I thought it over and then, after realizing that going into the kitchen to talk to Lisabeth would be a horrible way to spend the last few hours left of the night, I joined him.

Soon I found that his voice engulfed me and his laughter intoxicated me as we sat there, shooting the breeze about this, that, and the other thing. Denny was a college student studying to be a veterinarian. He loved animals—always had. He wasn't much deeper than that, but it was all right by me tonight. Tonight I could put my politics and other angry issues aside and bask in what I was quickly starting to believe was a little miracle—the thought that I would be happy again.

"I mean, I was raised on a farm. I guess I should love oil, too, but I've never seen a school that taught you how to fix oil problems," he said, causing me to burst into drunken laughter. I had been laughing at nothing for hours and felt giddy, as if I'd been drinking.

Too soon, it seemed, the parlor doors opened and the room began to empty its contents, drunk and happy. Molly noticed me and Denny visiting on the sofa, and I noticed her eyebrow rise. I knew she would have some words for me once the house emptied, and now she would have questions as well.

"Could I come calling on you, say, tomorrow evening or something?" Denny asked as he followed his parents to the door.

"I'm sure that would be all right. I mean, if I'm not grounded forever," I said.

Molly walked over to me. "You can come calling," she told him while standing behind me, stroking my hair lightly, resembling a caring mother.

As expected, Denny would drive his parents home, and all would sleep well that night, especially me— dreaming of my new boyfriend. There was something special about Denny to me. I don't know if I was just getting lonely or if I was forgetting Noah, but I didn't turn this boyfriend away. He was the first boy who wasn't trying to get into my blouse or my panties; he just seemed to like me for myself.

"So, looks like you and Denny Johnson are hitting it off pretty well," Molly said to me one night when I got in from another evening spent with him. It was early enough to be proper, so I was surprised she seemed to be waiting up. All had been forgiven with regard to that night I fought with Mary, at least on Molly's end. I'd yet to make it to the colored side of town to find Lisabeth and Mary, but I knew that soon I would.

"I like him enough," I answered.

She smiled and then said, "He's rich, you know."

Her statement shocked me. "Molly, I hope you don't think that I . . ." I began.

She raised her hand to quiet me, chuckling just a little at the irony of the situation. Without trying, I had snagged big game. "Denny's been talking to his parents about you. He really likes you, Em." Her words were starting to sound a little serious yet not intimidating. She sounded almost motherly in her tone. I took off my coat. Suddenly, she sighed heavily.

"Molly, what's wrong?" I asked, thinking she had bad news or perhaps an unreasonable request for me . . . like, "Marry Denny before the week is out, or we'll be out on the street." My stomach tightened at that thought. I liked Denny, but marrying him hadn't crossed my mind.

Then, as if she had finally decided something, she reached for a letter off a small table. "This came for you today," she told me.

The postmark sent my heart sailing. It was a letter from home. Ripping at it like a greedy animal, I tore at the envelope.

"It's from my cousin Josie." I exploded with excitement as I read the first few words. "Mary told her I was here and gave her the address." I giggled giddily, and then, as my eyes fell on the news from home, my sadness came in. Indeed, my mother had died. Aunt Rebecca had married up again and was living in Montgomery, Alabama, with her husband. Josie wasn't happy at all there with the city life and the restrictions that being around so many white people brought. Segregation was an ugly thing when in full bloom.

Josie went on to tell me how many resented the fact

that I had run off, leaving my mother there to die all alone. Josie didn't ask me anything about my life on the white side of the world, but I knew she wanted to ask. She spoke about Martin Luther King and his sermons. The Reverend Martin Luther King was all over the paper, and I was certain Josie was learning from him firsthand. She even surprised me with talk about the civil rights movement and some of the rallies she'd attended. She had joined the NAACP. I could tell by the way she tempered her words, she felt there was a separation between us now . . . one that went beyond miles. No doubt, Mary had told her how we met. What Mary said must have hurt her. I read faster now to see if there was any news about Noah, but there was none. But then again, why would Josie write of news of Noah? He was the love of my life, not hers.

"I'm going to write her back tonight," I said to Molly, folding the letter and tucking it deep into the waistline of my jeans. Molly stared at me, and then a slight smile broke her lips. She shook her head.

"No, Em. I can't allow it," she said.

I felt my face twist. "What?"

"You can't write her back. I only gave you that letter . . . Hell, I don't know why I gave it to you." Molly laughed now. It was a sad laughter, filled with mixed emotions. "But you can't write her. You can't mess this thing with Denny up."

"Oh, Molly, please. You can't keep me from the only family I have. You can't—"

"Look here, Em . . . the only family you have is standing right here in front of you, girl! You better recognize that and get your head on straight."

"Molly, but it's my family . . . my life," I tried to explain.

"It's your past, and you have to get over it and keep looking forward, Em. That summer you left Shreveport was your last colored summer. You follow me?"

Molly explained, holding me tightly by both arms. "Tomorrow we're having lunch with Denny's mother," she said then. "I didn't want to say anything, but it's been hard enough for me to cover over this fight you had with Mary. The Johnsons think you were just fighting with the help. Let's leave it at that."

I could barely hear her anymore as my mind went blank and my body ached all over.

Money does things to people. It changes them, and hardly ever for the better, in my opinion. It throws people into a game where the winners aren't really winners in the end. I'd never had money, but I'd lived long enough with Molly, pretending as though I did, and for a long time it was somewhat fun, but for some reason, with Meredith Johnson, it wasn't fun any longer. She was a vicious woman, materialistic and rude. I didn't like her much, and I could tell Molly didn't, either. I knew I had to stay in the game, though . . . for Molly's sake, so now the only question was, Would I play nice?

"So what part of Texas do you hail from?" Meredith asked, grinning while she spoke. She could tell my accent was no more Texan than French, and I wasn't sure of the answer she wanted. She had been asking me question after question about my background all afternoon. I felt as if she were choosing a dog and wanting to make sure of the breeding and pedigree, the purity of the blood, rather than a possible wife for her son.

I had accepted that this was where they expected things to go with me and Denny, whether we were ready or not.

"She's not from Texas. She's from St. Louis," Molly jumped in—again, answering for me. "She's my brother's child. I told ya'll that," Molly went on, urging Meredith to force her memory to go back to the imag-

...nary conversation that she had had once with her. Finally, Meredith shrugged casually, as if bored with naming yet another round of truth or dare with Molly.

"You already hire your help for your party?" Molly asked, getting Meredith on a subject she enjoyed, spending money and entertaining.

"Well, Molly, I was thinking. Maybe I could use your gals, Mary and Lisabeth, and they did such a wonderful job at your little party," she answered, paying Molly a sideways compliment. "I thought it would be wonderful to have a repeat, us all together again . . . of course, minus that little entertaining incident in the kitchen," she said, snorting with laughter. I simply wrinkled my nose, forcing a smile.

"Oh, Meredith, are you sure?" asked Molly, sounding forced before flashing me a quick wink.

"Well, yes," she answered, and then turning my face to hers, she nodded again. "Because my little Denny would have a fit if I had a party without his little Em there," she said, sounding as if she were speaking to an infant. Apparently, I had passed the test, impressing her with my mouth closed.

Chapter 13

The bus was full, but I knew I would get a seat. This wasn't Alabama, and I wasn't black . . . at least nobody knew I was. So I took a seat right up front with the other folks who thought they were better than everybody riding in the back. I hadn't thought about my seat on the bus before, but today it hit me hard.

I'd been writing Josie and receiving her letters at the Garcias' home. I would read them to Mr. and Mrs. Garcia, who enjoyed listening to me and my cousin's exchange. They could tell I was happy to hear from Josie, although they weren't quite sure why we were friends, as I edited the letters while I read, leaving out the parts that related us by our mothers.

When I stepped from the bus into colored town, all sorts of stares and quandaries greeted me. It was St. Louis all over again. Only this time I was ready for the Bickel-like reception, and it would be met by a new Emerald Jackson . . . one that wasn't gonna take that kinda shit . . . no way, no how.

I had Mary's address and headed right for her house on foot. I didn't bring my car for fear it would be stolen or that those who had nothing but resentment for me might do some other foul, hateful thing. I didn't stop for a minute to think about my own actions as being prejudiced. I just felt they were reasonable— considering what, I knew, many thought about whites in that neighborhood. I'd even worn a dress so as to maybe appear to be a social worker of some kind. There were many new programs coming up designed to help the poor, and maybe I would pretend to be a person involved in such a mission.

The door opened, and Mary all but did a double take when she saw me. "Girl, what choo want here?" she asked me, looking around suspiciously.

"I'm here to say I'm sorry and to thank you for locating Josie." I outstretched my hand.

"You don't sound sorry," she said. I smacked my lips and rolled my eyes. She was going to make this tough, I could tell.

"Look, you didn't get fired, did you? And Mrs. Johnson is planning to have you and Lisabeth serve at her party in a few weeks."

"Yeah, I know about that already. Lisabeth already called me."

"So there ya go." I grinned.

"You ain't had a dang thing to do with that, girl . . . so don't act like you did," Mary said, fighting a grin. "And just because I tow you up don't mean you have to come here and—"

"You didn't tear me up!"

"I'll do it again if you want me to," she threatened teasingly. I held up both hands in surrender. We both laughed. "You wanna come inside?" she asked me. Now I looked around, wondering if perhaps it was a trap. "Ain't nothing bad gonna happen to you."

"So are we friends?" I asked.

Mary shrugged. "Maybe."

I stepped into the house. It was humble but clean.

There were several children running around. "Where's your mother?"

"Working. She irons for this white lady downtown. Matter a fact, I need to get to work soon myself."

"Who watches the children?"

"My daddy," she answered, sounding a little defensive. Mary was an angry girl, I could tell. But she probably had her reasons. Looking around her home, I saw many unfamiliar symbols. Finally, curiosity got the best of me.

"What do those mean?" I pointed.

"I'm Muslim," she answered.

"Muslim?"

"Yeah, Muslim . . . I figure you don't know nothing about it. I bet you ain't ever even heard of Elijah Muhammad."

"No, I haven't," I answered. "I'd like to, though," I told her. She smiled.

"You couldn't handle it," she said, sounding a lot like Scott, another person who assumed I couldn't handle something. It was funny how little either of them knew about me and what I could handle.

"Try me," I challenged.

"Okay. Let's sit down, and I'll show you some of our literature." She pulled out several booklets, and we sat down and studied.

The night of the big shindig came. This was the event of the year in Dallas. Anyone who was important was planning on attending this gala. It was in all the local papers. Even the governor was coming.

I had never taken so long to get dressed in my life— looking myself over and over in that mirror, to make sure everything was right. I couldn't believe it was me. Looking back, Molly had worked her magic on me that night. I looked like the million bucks Molly had hoped she would end up with if me and Denny got hitched.

Denny's eyes lit up when we were announced at the door by their black butler. Even the butler looked me over out of the corner of his eye. Maybe he had seen me at Mary's house, or maybe he had been informed, or maybe it was the new way I looked at things after learning about the Muslims and the way they did things. Maybe I was a new me. . . .

I was perfect at dinner, having been groomed for this night. Every now and then, however, I would glance over at Molly, making sure to see her satisfaction and pleasure in me. I knew she was happy. I had snagged Denny Johnson without so much as a struggle. Strangely enough, the thought of marrying Denny didn't make me sick to my stomach. He wasn't so bad. If all went well, we would marry, and she would keep the ranch and her dignity. Brent had been calling lately. Perhaps the Holsted honeymoon had ended, and he was back to see whether Molly would stir it up for him. But the day he showed up, she had hid in the closet and had had me lie to him about not being home. I did it gladly.

Dinner had ended, and an interesting conversation between the governor and a couple of gentlemen had ensued. Oddly enough, they were discussing the civil rights movement—Martin Luther King, to be precise. I wanted to join in, but Denny stood and made an announcement.

"Now that you've stuffed us, me and my jewel are going for a walk," Denny announced, letting them in on his pet name for me. It was odd he had chosen to call me jewel over Emerald. Perhaps he wasn't sure about which gem to place with the color of my eyes, or perhaps it just hadn't dawned on him that perhaps Emerald was my real name . . . he was so much better with animals.

"Walk? Denny, it's freezing out there," Meredith

began, only to be shushed by Denny's father, who gave us a wink, while Denny helped me with my new coat.

"They'll be warm enough, Mother," Denny's father said. All the men in earshot chuckled. I glanced at Molly, who gave me a slight nod. I understood it as loud as if she had spoken. *You can show him the farm, but don't let him get the milk without buying the cow,* she said, with her eyes.

Denny's folks had built him a studio apartment out in back of their large home. His father had converted a hay barn on the property into an upstairs apartment, with an enclosed garage underneath. We went in. Sparsely furnished, the room had little warmth and was not very inviting. Denny removed my coat.

"Denny, I'm cold," I said, shivering now in the cold, sterile-feeling room.

"Not for long." He smiled, pulling me into an embrace. "May I kiss you?" he asked, holding my chin up so he could see my face.

This was our first kiss. Denny was such a gentleman. "Yes," I answered, just in time to feel his thin lips brush against mine lightly. Instead of the repulsion I thought I would feel, it was a rather pleasant kiss— almost polite.

The feeling gave me a flutter in my belly. It had been a lifetime since I'd felt a nice kiss—or so it seemed.

"If we were to marry, we'd have some beautiful children," he said now, still holding me close.

"Marry? Denny, we've just met," I said, standing back from him.

"I'm not saying we'll marry . . . I mean, not anytime soon," he added.

"Denny Johnson, are you asking me to marry you?" I asked, surprising myself with my own forwardness.

He blushed and stammered before finally regaining his confidence.

"Well, jewel, I'd say yes if that was what I was asking you," he answered, flashing a goofy grin. We kissed again. This time I could feel a bit more heat coming from him, a little more passion. My heart raced, but I beat it off so as not to be afraid of what might happen next between us. I thought of Molly's words and knew what I had to do to save her ranch.

I sat on the small sofa in the dark room while I allowed Denny to enjoy my lips and neck, and soon I felt his hands on the zipper of my beautiful dress. I moved away from him.

"No, Denny. You wouldn't want me all used up before our wedding night," I said, sounding coy and virginal. Little did Denny know, he was second to Noah, and no man would ever take Noah's place.

"Come on, Em. We're practically engaged. I just want to see what I'm getting. Let me just look at you naked. I promise I won't touch you."

"Denny . . . shame on you!" I scolded. "Now, you know your mother would skin you alive if she ever thought you spoke so indecently to me."

"Em, stop joking around. Everybody knows Molly is—"

"Not one word about Molly or this whole thing is off," I interjected quickly. He held up his hands.

"I'm sorry," he answered. "But your aunt is kinda loose. I mean, she has my mother doubting if being with you is good for me. I had to beg her to—"

"Then, Denny, maybe it's not," I explained. "There are a lot of things you don't know about me and . . ."

Just then, I could hear voices downstairs, in the garage. It was Denny's father and another man, whose voice I didn't recognize. They were speaking loudly, and I could hear them clearly. Their words were full of viciousness and bigotry. They were bad-mouthing the governor and his liberal views on segregation. They planned violence on one of the local Baptist churches. They spoke of hanging someone . . . murder. They spoke as if planning a social tea party, when, in fact, it was horrid acts of bloodshed against my people.

Denny, after hearing what I heard, put his finger to my lips and whispered to me to get my coat. I quickly obeyed, feeling my heart beating a mile a minute. I was torn. My first thoughts were to go down there and have it out with the men, but as I caught a glimpse of my petite stature in the mirror on Denny's wall, I opted against that move.

The door leading to the staircase was easy to find even in the dark, so out we went, closing it quietly behind us. We slipped by the open garage while hurrying back to the house, entering through the kitchen entrance. We both were out of breath when we entered.

"I thought he knew I was taking you there," Denny said about his father's intrusion downstairs. Mary and Lisabeth, caught off guard by our sudden entrance, stopped what they were doing.

"Denny, I can't believe what your father was saying. I can't believe what he's planning. He's going to hurt those people, Denny. You've got to tell somebody," I said. I was panicked and not thinking clearly. All I knew was we had to do something. We couldn't let what Denny's father was planning happen. "You know the governor! Talk to him. Tell him."

Denny's eyes were wide with mortification. I could tell he really didn't know what to do. He ran out of the kitchen, toward the living room. I started to follow, but Lisabeth grabbed my arm.

"His daddy's a Klansman. You besta tread carefully with that boy. He ain't never gonna turn on him. He'll turn on you first," she whispered and then went quickly back to cleaning the dishes. I looked at Mary, whose face showed nothing more than pure fear.

"Mary, they are talking about burning a church. He said . . . Howard, I think. Is there a pastor with that name?" I whispered, rubbing the goose bumps off my arms. Mary looked around at Lisabeth.

"Oh my God, yeah, I know Mr. Howard. Well, if you gonna try to stop them, you gonna have a fight on your hands. You want I should tell Luke? He's the pastor's son," Mary said.

"Denny will stop his father," I said, sounding confident. Lisabeth's head went back in laughter . . . mockery at my statement.

"Girl, you been white too long. You starting to believe them folks care about things like black folks," Lisabeth interjected acerbically.

"Lisabeth . . . we're not things. We're people," I said.

"We?" she laughed.

Just then, Molly came into the kitchen. Her eyes were wide with questions. "What's going on here, Em? You causing trouble again . . . My Lord, it's getting so I can't take you anywhere anymore. Denny just ran through the house like it was on fire and told everyone good night."

"Good night?" I gasped. Lisabeth laughed, and this time Mary did, too.

"Looks like Em was fightin' again," Mary said.

"I was not!" I yelped. Mary caught my eye, and I realized then, she knew what she was saying and I was to go along.

"Girl be fightin' all the time. That Denny's got a tiger on his hands," Lisabeth said and chuckled. "Denny'll get over it."

Molly scowled. "Em! Please now . . . you have to stop being difficult."

"I'm sorry. Do you want me to apologize to him?" I

said, acting as if I was going to head straight for Denny's bedroom. "He was getting a little fresh with me and so—"

"No! Of course not. Meredith is already in there . . . She could see he was upset. I suggest we get out of here."

"Okay," I said, giving Mary a quick wink, hoping she realized that it was a sign that I would be showing up later that night, determined to help out my people. I was determined for this to be my last night being used for the color of my skin. It was time I started using the color of my skin for my own benefit. If this didn't prove my loyalty to my race, I didn't know what would.

The occasion to stand up for right came within a few days of overhearing Denny's father.

I hadn't said anything to Denny about my feelings on the matter of his father's affiliation with the Klan. As a matter of fact, I hadn't said anything to Molly, either. I was fuming inside and knew better than to cross that bridge with anyone, especially anyone white. I felt funny leaving Molly out of my plans, but I couldn't trust her to go along with me. It was dangerous what I was planning. I didn't want to put Molly at risk, and I didn't want Molly to take me out of the game.

Denny and I had spent the day together, talking about the mating rituals of eagles. Denny found that topic arousing, and so perhaps he thought I would, too. There was something about the way they risked death to copulate that he found very exciting.

"I would risk death to make love to you," he said, kissing my neck between each word. I just smiled and stroked his brow.

"I'm sure you would, but for now, we can't be naughty. Besides, I'm not that kind of girl." I giggled shamelessly.

I wanted information, and I was gonna give up my virtue if it meant getting it. For that, I was prepared.

"But I want to get naughty with you." He giggled. I hated when he talked that baby talk to me. It made my skin crawl a little bit, but I had to figure that he felt he was being sexy.

"Where would we do it?" I asked him.

"My room, where else?"

"In the house? How could we possibly do it there with your daddy home?"

"My daddy ain't home. He's out with his friends. They're running errands." He snickered.

"Ohhh, I see."

"He won't be in until after midnight . . . drunkerin' a skunk, no doubt."

"Don't your mama mind all his running the streets?" I asked, running my fingers through his hair.

"I wouldn't call it running the streets. I'd call it more of a mission . . . but now, why we worrying about my daddy and his clan?"

I tried not to flinch when he used the word *clan*. I'm sure he meant one thing, but I knew, in reality, it meant another.

"Where does he hang out?"

"Look, sweetie," Denny said, pulling me up to my feet. "Stop worrying. Daddy won't be home for a while . . . Let's just say, he's at church, and with all he's got to pray over, he'll be tied up a while."

I knew it! He was about to burn a church.

I had to get out of there.

"Okay, Denny," I told him. "Tell you what . . . Let me go home, and I'll tell Molly something to get out of the house, and then I'll meet you at your room upstairs later. How's that?"

"Perfect." He grinned. "And you're perfect," he said, kissing me. I remember how I didn't close my eyes during the kiss, as I was only thinking about getting to the police.

Being a white female had its advantages where the police were concerned; at least that was my humble opinion. I found I could walk in, hold my head up high, tattletale on someone, and walk out . . . without so much as leaving my name. And guess what? They acted on my report.

Denny's father and his friends were thwarted in many of their plans to wreak havoc on the black community.

I would tease Denny, and he would tell me what I needed to know. And I did it all without having to give up an ounce of my virtue.

In just those few months since making that eye contact with Mary, we had squashed several attempts by Denny's father to do damage to the black churches in the area, including one of the Muslim temples. I had impressed Mary with my loyalty so much so that she had agreed to allow Josie to come stay with her for a while as soon as I got the money together to send for her.

I was ecstatic.

The fact that I was using Denny against his father and, in fact, playing with fire never crossed my mind.

Until I got burned.

Chapter 14

The last patron finally left the diner, and I let out a sigh. Right as I locked the door, I saw the ball of dust speeding toward the diner. I watched as the young motorcyclist parked and climbed off his bike as if it were a stallion. As he strolled toward the door I recognized his casual stride, but it was only when he pulled off the helmet that I realized it was Scott Baker. I hadn't seen him in ages. As a matter of fact, he looked different, tan and weathered. I unbolted the door.

"Hey, doll," he greeted.

I tried to hide my excitement over seeing him, but I couldn't. "Scott! Where in the wide world have you been?"

"Hollywood, doll. I'm a movie star now."

"Get outta town!" I chuckled. "In motion pictures?"

"Yeah. I'm what they call a body double. I do all the falling and jumping for bigger names. It's a living," he said, showing pride in his accomplishments.

"Is Hollywood wonderful?"

"You betcha."

"Well, what brings you here?"

"You. I wanted to see you."

I felt the heat rush to my face and hid it by running the towel over a table and otherwise looking distracted. I couldn't help it. Scott was gorgeous. After setting his helmet on the counter and then pulling off his leather jacket, he wore only a white T-shirt, which exposed many more muscles than I ever remembered him having. Before I knew it, he had pulled me in tight and kissed me. This time I kissed him back. There was nobody in the diner, so I have to admit I kissed him back a couple of times and even ran my hands along his taut arms. Denny was nowhere on my mind.

Scott stayed for over an hour, while we talked. The sun had set, and darkness was coming in.

"Look here, I'ma go see my daddy, and I'll stop by later, okay? You gonna wait for me, or do you want me to come out to the ranch?"

"Nooo, not the ranch," I said, thinking of how Molly would flip if Scott pulled up on that motorcycle of his, calling on me.

"I see I'm still as welcome as ever."

I chuckled. "Scott, it's not the same anymore. I'm not the same anymore. We need to talk. Come here later. I'll wait."

"Sure, doll. You're right. We need to talk. I've learned some things while in Hollywood," he said, flashing a million-dollar smile while sliding his sunglasses back on and shrugging into a hot-looking leather jacket. He could have easily been the next James Dean.

Scott came out to the diner every day, right before closing. I had told him I was engaged, but it didn't seem to matter to him.

"When am I gonna meet this so called fiancé?" he asked me while slurping the last of his malt.

Joe, one of my favorite dinner patrons, overheard

and got in on the conversation. "Whaddaya wanna meet that joker for? You gonna fight 'em?" he asked.

Scott laughed. "Nah, just wanna see the man who beat me out for the jewel," Scott joked.

"Yeah, she sure is a looker, huh?" Joe added, the two of them speaking as if I weren't standing there, listening.

"Stop it, you guys. You gonna give me a big head," I gushed.

Scott laughed out loud. "Get a big head?" he teased.

"I like this guy, Emmy. Why not dump bird boy for him? He's a hunk," Joe said, winking at me.

"Because I'm not available," I explained. I figured by claiming Denny, it would cover all my bases. I would be safe, in case he had any spies out, and I would protect myself from temptation. Scott's presence had given me thoughts I'd not had in a long time. I knew, soon he'd be talking about heading back to California. I didn't want to hear that, and so I figured by protecting my feelings, by keeping things light between us, my heart would be safe.

We'd taken in a movie once or twice since he'd been back, but no petting or even another kiss had passed between us. I was being a good girl . . . for the first time in my life.

Joe finally left, and I finished clearing off the last of the tables.

The dinner crowd had been thick that day, and I thought it would never thin out. The holiday weekends were always this way. Folks loved Molly's diner and Mrs. Garcia's Tex-Mex special. Mrs. Garcia had taken over the cooking a long time back, and folks just wanted to kill for it. Even if Molly lost the ranch, she would still be okay keeping the diner. But losing the ranch was not an option anymore, in my opinion—nor a worry. I had Denny hooked and wasn't going to mess that up. I was only after Denny's father. In my mind, I could separate the two very easily.

Mrs. Garcia had gone home already. Seeing as how I had Scott lingering, she figured I would be safe enough.

"Emmy, I want to ask you something," Scott began right before the phone rang. While I went to answer it, he put a nickel in the jukebox.

"So, when do you get off, baby?" Denny asked me when I picked up the phone.

"Soon," I told him, while wiping off the counter where I stood.

"You are such a wonderful woman. So pure and good . . ." he began. My heart began to grow heavy. If only Denny knew the truth about me. I was none of those things. I was a liar. I was a user. I was a black woman. I was black, and his father was a Klansman. We were no more suited for each other than—well, than darkness and light.

"No, Denny, I'm not," I began. He shushed me. I wanted to give Denny a chance. I wanted to give us a chance, but I didn't know how it would work out, unless he got some backbone and stood up to his father, and there didn't seem to be any chance of that happening. I'd given him many opportunities to step up to the plate and protest his father's actions. But he'd not done it, nor had he seemed bothered by his father's blocked attempts to terrorize innocent people. I knew Mr. Johnson was getting frustrated; I could see it on his face every time I came to the house. He was grumpy and unfriendly. Maybe I was rubbing it in by being extra smiley when in his presence, but it made me happy deep inside to know I had a part in making him miserable. Standing up to his father would surely prove Denny's love to me, and often I eased onto the topic of the plans that we'd overheard that night, but Denny would simply change the subject.

"Well, jewel, tonight I have some business to take care of. I need to straighten out some things with my father," he said. "But after that, I'll come by the ranch. It'll be late, so you better warn Molly so she won't have the Mexican shoot me."

I hated when he called Mr. Garcia that. "Mr. Garcia would never do that." I laughed, sounding fake and forced.

"You never know what people do when they don't want to show their real feelings."

"What does that mean?"

"Just saying, sometimes people will stand behind others when they don't want to show who they truly are."

I thought about the ugly caps and the pointed headpieces worn by the Klansmen. "Yes, I agree," I said.

"I thought you would. Well, jewel . . . my sweet jewel, I'll see you later tonight."

"Until then, Denny," I said, hanging up. He sounded strange, but I let it go, realizing I had wiped over the same spot on the counter this whole time.

When I hung up, Scott came over to where I stood. He held out his hand. "I think you owe me this dance." "Love me Tender" by Elvis Presley was on the jukebox; it was one of my favorites. Scott pulled me into his arms, and we swayed back and forth, making a tight circle, as I laid my head on his shoulder. Scott was a good dancer, and I regretted not having enjoyed dancing with him sooner.

I could imagine myself with Scott. We were compatible in a way, him and me. I didn't realize it then, but I do now.

Lifting my chin, he kissed me.

"I better get going, doll," he said after I opened my eyes.

"Yeah, you better," I said, allowing a lovelorn sigh to escape my lips.

"But I'm gonna be back and . . ." He paused. "Nah, I won't say it."

"Tell me," I urged, playfully pinching his rib cage. He feigned pain and then raised his hand.

"Okayyyy. I'm gonna be back and ask you something," he said.

"What! What!" I giggled. He shook his head, shrugging into his jacket and heading out.

Leaning against the door, I watched him pull off into the darkness. It was funny how Scott had affected me, how he looked at me. It was as if he knew the truth. Maybe he had met people like me there in Hollywood. I'd heard about many colored people passing for white in California.

Maybe Scott and I would leave together. Maybe he would take me there, and I would find people like me, living in the shadows of their former selves. Maybe I would find a place to truly fit in. Where life wasn't just always so black or white. Hollywood.

How I had dreamed of that place. It was where television was made. And how I loved television . . .

I started away from the door but then remembered I hadn't bolted it. Turning back, I saw a sight that would always stay in my mind and heart . . . I knew the moment I saw the hooded men, I would never forget this moment. Even if I died this day, I would roll over in my grave, disturbed by the memory of the men in the white caps. I screamed.

"Nigger lover!" one of them said before slugging me hard in the face. I fell and hit my head on the table's edge.

Before losing consciousness, I heard someone call

out. "Jewel! Larry, you lied! You said we were only going to scare her!"

It was Denny. I was barely conscious, but I knew his voice, even though, among all the hooded men, I could not see his face.

"Stay out of it, boy, or die with her!" the big one said before tossing the burning branch toward the counter, which quickly ignited. I couldn't scream. It would have taken too much energy. I was fighting too hard to stay conscious, and it wasn't working very well. I might have been mistaken, but I thought I heard Elvis start to play on the jukebox. My mind soared, and I imagined myself cutting a rug with Scott. Swinging around and around, smiling, laughing . . .

The smoke was choking me and the voices were muffled now while they bashed and broke up Molly's diner. Unable to feel my legs, I knew I was gonna die here tonight. I tried to move my mouth to call out Denny's name, but it didn't come . . . At least I don't think it did. I don't know how long I lay in that fire, but I figured I was dead, so what did it matter?

"Doll!" I heard after what seemed like forever. I tried to open my eyes to see my savior, but before I could, the weight of the leather covered my face, and I felt my limp body being lifted and carried. The cool air hit my legs, and I knew we had to be outside. Laying me on the ground, Scott pulled the jacket off my face. "You're safe now, doll. Wake up! Wake up!" he screamed. As I opened my eyes, they met his. I know I smiled at him, because he smiled back.

The crack of the gun blast shocked me more than the fact that he'd been shot. The bullet hit him in the back. It came from the darkness, and to this day I'll never know who pulled that trigger. Perhaps it had been Denny, lurking in the bushes, waiting to see if I was really dead. Maybe it was his father. . . .

Chapter 15

Scott's funeral was small. It wasn't as if Scott's father knew any of his new Hollywood friends, even though I'm sure he was missed on his job. I could barely stand to see the old man there crying while holding on to Scott's younger siblings. I kept swallowing hard to keep down my words. How I wanted to say so much more than simply "I'm sorry."

It was never established who was behind the gun that killed Scott Baker. But it was never disputed that he saved my life that night.

He was a true rebel, and I had become his cause.

Chapter 16

Fortunately, the insurance policy on Molly's diner paid out quickly, which was not the case for the owners of the churches and the black home owners, who waited . . . devastated, having had their dreams go up in flames . . . dozens since that night. The Klansmen seemed to be on a mission to punish everyone I knew, and that included Mary and Lisabeth, who quickly packed up and moved to Alabama, barely escaping with their lives.

The police did nothing to stop the short raid on the colored folks and, blinded, went on about business as usual, as if the burning of the diner and the burning of the churches and homes of those innocent people didn't tie in together. It all sickened me. I couldn't even eat and soon took to my bed, ill.

Not to my surprise, Denny broke up with me and, taking his parents' advice, left for college in Connecticut, without even so much as a good-bye. Good riddance, I say. I heard that within just a few months, he married some rich socialite. His story would have ended happily ever after if, while on a hunting expedition, he hadn't been killed by a brown bear. I always felt he should have stuck with healing animals instead of hunting them.

For weeks after Scott's death, Molly tried to get me back to normal. But it just wasn't happening. I was despondent, and according to the doctor, mentally broken. I didn't see why I had been allowed to continue to walk around, while Scott, who had had a real life, had to lay in the ground. None of it made sense to me.

I often wondered about my life and how different it would have been had I been allowed to be black. The thought would often hit my funny bone . . . I mean, seriously thinking about it, how much worse could it have been than what it was. I was starting to think that I was just a jinx: I was a walking black cloud.

As many times as I thought about my mother's loving words to me before she died, perhaps it was my aunt's words that spoke the truth. Perhaps she was right about me being cursed. Maybe it was best that Noah had never found me, for whatever happiness he had found in life, I would, surely, be the reason he lost it.

Mr. Garcia met me at the stable while I strolled between the two horses Molly had managed to hang on to. The money was thin but not gone, and she was determined to maintain the ranch to the bitter end.

"So how are you feeling today?" Mr. Garcia asked me in Spanish.

"Low," I answered truthfully. I spoke in Spanish also.

"Why? You're young. The day is for the young. You need to be dancing. It's a Friday night."

"Mr. Garcia, I will never dance again. Life is bad for me," I told him, handing the horse some straw.

"Bad? You haven't even lived it yet."

"Mr. Garcia, you just don't know me as well as you think you do. I've had seven lifetimes already. . . ."

"But seven means perfection. You're on the right track."

"Seven is also craps, and that's what my life has been . . . craps."

"What do you know about that? You sound like the old men who sit around the saloon."

"I feel old."

"But you are not old. You've not begun to live."

"I've lived and lost. You know, I should have died in that fire. But, instead, a boy saved me, and he died. I'll never forget that or get over it."

"I'm not saying you should, but you need to look deeper into what happened that night. Find a way to live through it, not over it." He smiled and strolled back toward his house.

Get through life, not over it. . . .

I felt my back straighten just a little as his words rolled around in my head like an aspirin, easing my pain just a little. I was black and had been trying my damnedest to get over that fact for years now. It was the reason for everything that I'd been going through in life, so why defeat my purpose for being by trying to avoid it? I needed to go home, face my demons, get through them, and stop trying to get over them.

It was late when I finished packing. I knew Molly was asleep. Slipping out the back, I loaded up my car. I glanced around once or twice as I felt watched, but no one appeared, and so I finished my escape.

Maybe it had been Mr. Garcia spying me that night, and maybe he was smiling, knowing he had emboldened me to push forward on my quest to find myself, to get this thing called life going, and maybe in the process, to get the young woman named Emerald back.

Chapter 17

I didn't know where Montgomery, Alabama, was, but I was on my way there. I knew exactly what I was going to do when I got there, too. Maybe I wouldn't get arrested for sitting on a bus or drinking out of a whites-only fountain, but I was ready to fight for the cause of black people. Maybe I would become a Muslim, who knew, but I was ready. I had money, a car, and the address of my family—well, of Rebecca and Josie—but that was the best I could do. It was all I had, and I would work through that, too, as there was no getting over Aunt Rebecca.

The letters from Josie had stopped coming a long time ago, and I knew it was because I had stopped answering them a long time ago. Maybe Mary had told her what had happened, and Josie had grown scared of me . . . who knew, but I was going to find out.

I'd driven for two days before realizing I was headed in the wrong direction. Perhaps it was the way the sun reflected off the red clay of the adobe houses that gave me a clue.

"New Mexico," I yelled, slamming my head on the hood of the car.

"Where did you think you were?" the gas station attendant asked me.

"I thought I was . . ." I fell silent. "What does it matter?" I sighed, looking around at all the desert that lay for miles in front of me.

What was I going to do in New Mexico? What was going to happen to me here? I shuddered at the thought as the little town came alive right before my eyes. However, it was when I heard the rooster crowing that I knew I was in trouble.

"Are you a movie star?" he asked me.

I felt my face frown up. "No. Why would you ask me that?"

"Many movie stars come through. They are usually drunk when they start out, and by the time they get sober, they find themselves here."

"No! I'm not drunk or a movie star. Gosh. Where can I find a room to rent or a hotel or . . ." I was whiny now and just wanted to roll up in a ball and cry. Just then I noticed a diner. It reminded me of Molly's place, and I was drawn to it.

Inside, the busy customers were eating their hurried meals, no doubt trying their best to finish so that they could get outta this place. I, too, wanted to leave but had no place to go. There was no way I was turning around and getting even more lost trying to get back. With my luck, I'd end up in hell before I made it back to Texas, and as I looked around at all the desert folks, dirty and dusty, I had to wonder if I hadn't landed there already.

"What'll it be?" the girl behind the counter asked me. She wore a name tag, which identified her as Cookie. She looked about my age, but with more sophistication behind her eyes. The longer I looked at her, the more she resembled Marilyn Monroe.

"I don't know." I sighed, sliding up to the counter.

"How about some coffee to start?" she asked. I agreed, smoothing my hair behind my ear.

"Where ya headed?" she asked, sliding the cup to me. I reached in my pocket for a dime but she stopped me.

"It's on me."

"Gee, thanks."

"Where you headed?" she asked again.

"I thought I was on my way to Alabama, but it seems I have no sense of direction. I left Texas about two days ago and ended up here."

The man next to me overheard and smiled into his cup, attempting to hold back laughter.

"Stop laughin', Pete. Maybe it's fate. Kismet," Cookie said, with a grin parting her full lips. "You see, I was headed to Las Vegas once and ended up here myself. That was, what, nearly five years ago now."

"Oh my God!" I groaned.

"Look, it's not that bad here. And if you don't have any plans, maybe you could come on to my place after my shift, get a good night's sleep, and . . ." She chuckled. "Maybe get your hands on a compass and start over."

I had to laugh. Cookie was right. It had to be my lack of sleep that was to blame for most of my navigational issues. I was sure of it now.

Cookie lived with two other girls, Sade and Marge. All of them looked like starlets, and I had to wonder what they were doing in this small town. Being as I felt like I had no choice, I was just going along with the flow. I still wanted to find my family, but destiny was taking me farther west.

"We go to college here," Cookie said.

"College?" I asked.

"Yeah, silly Willy, education. You know, using our brains and all that," Cookie said.

"I know what an education is," I answered quickly. "I love learning. I just never thought about going to college."

"Well, it's the thing to do if you wanna snag a man," Sade finally confessed.

"Now the cat's out of the bag," Cookie said and giggled.

"You go to school to learn in order to get married and lose . . ." I began.

"Lose what? Marriage and an education, it's a win-win situation," Marge said.

"For who?" I asked, thinking about all the wives I'd seen all my life—stifled and repressed, for the most part. And, I would never forget Greta, the epitome of a life interrupted.

"How old are you?" Cookie asked me.

"Twenty . . . no, twenty-one," I lied, not actually knowing at that moment. I'd lied about my age for so long. Who had kept count of the years? "What year is this?"

Cookie burst into laughter. "I like this girl."

As fate would have it . . . or kismet, as Cookie would put it, I landed a job at the diner and lived with the girls in their tiny house. I shared a room and, until I could afford my own, a bed with Sade. The bills went from being split in thirds to fourths. My having a car led to many fun Friday nights cruising the streets of Albuquerque, the neighboring city. It was an interesting few months, learning the culture of the people there. It was different from any place I had ever been before, or maybe it was just me, as it felt strange being in a place where no one asked anything of me but my friendship and maybe a few laughs. Cookie and Marge were on a perpetual manhunt, but it seemed as though Sade was more content. At least that was how it seemed until Valentine's Day rolled around. By then, I had lived in Albuquerque for six months.

"I am gonna go all the way with Bill tonight. I've thought about it for weeks, and, yep, I'm gonna do it," Cookie said, putting the final touches on her hair.

"You act like going all the way with somebody is news," Marge said teasingly.

"I'm a virgin . . . cut it out," Cookie protested. We all groaned. I must have groaned the loudest as she veered her next question to me. "So, Miss Mystery woman, what about you? You ever go all the way?"

"When I got married," I answered quickly.

"Ohhh, well, that answers one of my questions," Marge said. "But, of course, it leads to many more, but go on."

"No, I got married years ago."

"Couldn't have been too many years. You're just a kid now."

"Well, it wasn't legal. It was with a boy from my hometown," I said carefully. I'd been trained to speak without saying a whole lot. "We thought we were in love, so we got . . . married," I explained simplistically.

"But you weren't in love?" Sade asked me.

"Yes, we were." When I said the words, I noticed sadness come into Sade's eyes, but I didn't know why.

"Do you still love him?" Sade asked.

"I don't know. I guess . . . yes. But I'll never see him again, so it doesn't matter."

"If you did, would you go all the way again?" Cookie asked, sounding goofy and already drunk on the thought of having sex.

"In a heartbeat," I answered, bringing howls from both her and Marge . . . but not Sade.

We all took off for the local bar we hung out in, and within moments, Marge and Cookie disappeared, leaving Sade and me at the booth.

"What's got you like a mummy tonight?" I asked Sade. She smacked her lips and then, almost as if she was upset, she pulled out a small ring box and handed it to me.

"What's this?" I asked, opening the box.

"I was going to give it to you at home, but the time never got right. It's a Valentine's gift. I bought it for you," she answered. Needless to say, I quickly closed the box . . . speechless. I looked around, hoping nobody had seen the exchange between us. I didn't understand what was happening, and so I didn't want to share the moment before I knew what it was.

"Sade, why would you buy me a ring?"

"Because I love you."

"You don't love me, like this," I said, holding up the box. "It's not normal."

"It's normal for me."

"But not for me. Here . . ." I said, sliding the ring box back to her. My mind went to all the nights we'd slept in the same bed when I first arrived. How many times she'd seen me in my underthings, or worse . . . naked. How long I had avoided the advances of men, only to be trapped and made vulnerable by a woman. I didn't know what to do or say. It was always so much easier to reject the male advances, but here I was, unable to think on my feet. The music had turned from perky to dirgelike, the smoky room was choking me, and I needed air. I got up and went outside. Sade followed me. We got in the car. The silence was thick between us. Starting the engine, I drove. I figured maybe we would just clear the air, and that would be the end of it. Finding a nice place to park, I shut the car off.

"Can I at least kiss you?" Sade asked after a moment or two longer in silence. I turned to her.

"Sade, look . . . this isn't going to work, you and me.

I don't understand what's going on here. I mean, sure, I love you, too. I love all you gals. It's been great living with ya'll and—"

"I love the way you talk." Sade smiled. "I love to watch your lips move. I love everything about you. Sometimes at night I watch you sleep," she confessed. Her words came caught up in tears. "Please just let me kiss you, and I promise I won't say anything more about it, and I won't even ask you to wear the ring."

I stared at her for a long time, wondering how my kiss could help her. Would it help her? Was it the right thing to do? She wanted it so badly; I could see it in her eyes. She reminded me of Mr. Griffith . . . how he needed that kiss from me that night and I denied him.

Closing my eyes, I leaned in to receive Sade's soft lips on mine. I refused to kiss her back, but she didn't seem to care. Parting my lips with her tongue, she enjoyed my mouth. Soon her hand wandered and found itself on my breast, where she fondled the front of my sweater until my nipple hardened enough for her to tug.

"Can I touch your skin?" she asked.

"No."

"Then will you touch me?"

"Sade, this has gone too far already," I told her. "I feel dirty and this isn't right."

Pulling up her skirt, she slid her hands down her underpants and began to fondle herself. "Fine. I'll do it myself," she said, leaning back against the car door. I turned my head while she masturbated. "Please let me touch you," she begged all the while.

"No," I told her, without looking in her direction. I could hear her crying, but I still refused to give in to what I felt to be unnatural. As hard as Sade tried, she could not arouse me. Not even when she took her hairbrush out of her purse and proceeded to use it as if it was a male organ did I feel anything but pity for her. Finally, she was finished and ready to go back to the bar. I could tell she was embarrassed, and I felt terrible for her when she jumped out of the car and stormed back into the bar.

I sat in the car for a moment or two, wondering if I had done someone wrong. Maybe I should have allowed her to touch me. What could be so wrong with that? It wasn't as if I had to enjoy it.

Sade was my friend. I should have let her touch me.

What was I thinking? Again, I was allowing the wrong value system to rule me. "Hell, no! She cannot touch me like that. I don't even let men touch me like that. Damn, Em . . . Where is your marbles?" I asked myself.

Going inside, I looked for Sade but couldn't find her. Eventually, I spied Cookie and Marge; both had struck out in the man department.

"Where have you and Sade been?" Cookie asked. I felt the heat come up on my face. Apparently, neither of them knew of Sade's sexual preference, or maybe they did and felt it was normal or okay.

"Where is Sade now?" I asked, ignoring Cookie's question. We all looked around but didn't see her. Cookie went and asked the bartender. When she came back, she was grinning.

"Well, according to the bartender, she left with Johnny," Cookie said.

"Johnny? You're kidding? Sade hates that guy," said Marge.

"Apparently, not anymore."

"Who's Johnny?" I asked.

"Just the horniest man on earth," Marge added.

"He's awful . . . and he smells," Cookie went on.

"You think everybody smells," Marge told her. They

broke into laughter. I didn't seen anything funny and worried about Sade the rest of the night.

Lying in my bed, I couldn't sleep until I heard the door open and Sade come home. I jumped up and ran into the living room.

"What do you want?" she slurred.

"Are you okay?"

"What the hell do you care?"

"I care."

"No, you don't care. Nobody does. Nobody cares or understands. Nobody knows what it's like to live a lie every day of your life. To pretend that you are something when, in fact, you are something else."

"Oh, Sade, you just don't know how much I understand that," I told her.

"You can't understand. You like men. You can't possibly understand," she growled, attempting to keep her voice down. "Again tonight I tried. I tried to be normal," she went on. "I let that man crawl all over me and hump me like some dog in heat. I let it happen to prove that I was normal, and you know what? I threw up . . . all over his fuckin' bed." Sade burst into laughter.

"Sade . . . I . . ."

She held up her hand. "Just leave me alone. I'll sleep out here on the sofa."

"It's your room. You go to bed. I'll sleep out here."

"Why can't we just sleep in there together like it's always been, Emma?" she whined.

"You know I can't do that, Sade. I can't."

Sade's pleading face dropped, and she looked defeated. I couldn't look at her anymore and simply went back to bed, only to toss and turn all night in troubled sleep.

Cookie's bloodcurdling scream woke me . . . Hell,

it woke everybody in the neighborhood, I'm sure. Syd, the man next door, burst in without even knocking.

"What's happened!" he yelled.

"Sade, she's killed herself . . . in the bathroom. She cut her wrists!" Cookie cried.

Chapter 18

Sade's parents came after only a day. That's when I learned the house we all lived in belonged to Sade's parents. It didn't feel right to stay there, even though they had said we all could. I never told the others what had happened between Sade and me the night she killed herself, and so I felt too guilty to accept the offer. Many times over the weeks to come, Cookie and Marge would ask why Sade had taken her own life, what would have made her do it, and I, liar that I had grown to be, would just shrug my shoulders. I had deluded myself into thinking I was protecting Sade from the shame, when, in fact, I didn't want to face the fact that if I had only allowed her to touch me, she might still be alive. I think I knew that wasn't true, either. In my heart, I knew that was just another excuse to be unhappy.

Maybe Sade and I were more alike than I wanted to accept. We were both oddities under our skin. Deep inside, where nobody could see, we were different from everybody else, alone on a planet full of strangers. But the problem with that was that I think we both were looking for someone else to blame for what was not our fault, forgetting that other issue wasn't anyone else's fault, either. Nonetheless, Sade was right about one thing: no matter how much we tried to fit in, we just never seemed to be able to.

I grew a little angry when I thought about Sade too long. For when Sade took her life, she left me bearing a bigger responsibility to people like us, a responsibility to make this odd life work . . . to get through it.

"Where are you gonna go?" Cookie asked me, maybe hoping in a way that I would name a place she, too, was interested in going.

"I don't know. I thought I would go home, but then I realized"—I chuckled sardonically—"I don't really have one."

"E, I know we never really talked about stuff like this, but . . . are you in any kind of trouble?"

"Trouble?" I thought immediately about Mr. Griffith; I thought about Scott; I thought about Sade. I'd say I was in trouble. But now to whom I was accountable was still up to debate. My guess was that I was indebted to God, for he was the only one who really knew the truth about it all. But I had turned away from him in anger, and I had blasphemed so many times against his face . . . Surely, if my life was in his hands, it seems as though this life would have ended a while back, yet it continued . . . year after year.

I thought about my mother suddenly, thinking that maybe she was in heaven now, thinking that maybe she was there pleading my case before the Lord. I could hear her now, explaining how it had been her fault that all this mess had happened. I could hear her now, explaining how she would be more than willing to take on full responsibility for her wayward child, left on earth to flounder. I could just hear her telling the Almighty that despite her good intentions, I had deviated from the plan, which she thought was so simple. *Just be white*, she had asked of me . . . *and life will be so easy.* No, the signs that segregated were simple, the laws that prohibited me from crossing the race lines were simple . . . What faced me in the mirror every morning was as complicated as hell. Rubbing my forehead, I looked Cookie straight in the eyes before answering.

"No, not really," I answered vaguely. She gulped slightly, as if the answer wasn't quite what she had expected from an innocent-looking girl like me.

"Then I say, let's get this show on the road," she blurted.

"What?"

"I'm up for it."

"Up for what?"

"Whatever trouble you're in, I'm up for it. I knew the day I met you my life would change and, boy . . . has it ever. Where you go, I wanna go, E. I wanna be a part of what you're going through."

"Ohhh, no, you don't." I laughed.

"You're so very different. I don't know if you realize it, but you are. You're cool and well . . . different. I mean, I know you're a girl and all, but you just don't worry about the stupid stuff most girls do. You're focused and mature, and like now, you didn't even seem shook about what Sade did. It was like you'd seen that kind of thing before. You're like"—Cookie hunted for the word—"you're like a soldier."

I laughed out loud. If only she knew the war that waged in my life. A soldier . . . what an understatement.

"Well, I was just gonna drive until my car conked out and then—"

"Okay! Let's go!"

I laughed again and shook my head, going back to the room I'd shared with Sade until that fateful night. I had already packed my bags but had yet to put them in the car, so now I waited until Cookie threw together a few things, and off we went, headed north—I think.

Chapter 19

On December 20, 1957, Elvis Presley was drafted. My heart nearly broke. What was I to do without him? Despite all that had being going on in my life, I still depended heavily on the King to get me through. Oh well, the next phenom to come on the scene was Chuck Berry . . . at least in my book, and soon I was swinging with the best of them in Las Vegas, Nevada. Music had become my saving grace. Without it, I would have truly lost my mind.

Soon Cookie and I had landed jobs as cigarette girls at the El Rancho Hotel. It was a great job, and we got all the free smokes we wanted. Lounge music wasn't quite my speed, but Cookie enjoyed it and often would get caught standing still, watching the performer on stage. I knew she wanted to get up there and take the microphone herself. And she had a lovely voice. I'm sure given half a chance, she would have become a star. But not me. I couldn't carry a tune to save my life and was glad it never came up.

Vinny was a bouncer there at the hotel. He was big and intimidating, and worst of all . . . he liked me.

"Hey there, green eyes," he called to me as Cookie and I came through the back door . . . late again.

Getting to bed early was hard to do in a town that never slept. "Hey, Vin, you got us covered, right?" I called to him, clicking my teeth and making a pistol out of my finger and thumb. He just grinned and nodded goofily.

In addition to clubbing, I might add that Cookie opened my eyes to something new—reefer. Somehow Cookie's smoking pot made getting to work on time a bit more difficult, too. I don't know where Cookie got them or if she had always smoked them, but if she had, she never told me until we became roommates.

The first time I tried one was on a dare. She and I were sitting up in our small apartment, bored and hot. She disappeared into her room and came back out with a small cigar box.

"Ever smoke?" she asked me.

"I smoke all the time," I smarted off, holding out my cigarette, as if to say . . . "duh." She giggled.

"No, reefer . . . You ever smoke it?" she asked.

"No," I gasped, sitting forward in the big chair I was in, to get a better look when she opened the box. I'd never seen marijuana before. I was sure of it. But then again, maybe I had . . . who knows what grew on Molly's property.

Cookie quickly lit up her marijuana cigarette and took a long draw off of it and then passed it to me. "I dare you," she said.

I looked at her. I'm sure my eyes were filled with questions.

Where did you get this? How long have you been smoking it? Is this what you and Madge did in your room while Sade had other plans for me in our room?

The drug had an immediate affect, and I was giggled at nothing within just a few moments. The high took away all my other thoughts and filled my head with cartoon ones in their place. For me, however, not thinking clearly was a disadvantage, as thinking with nothing altering my brain was hard enough, so after trying it a few more times, I abandoned it. But not Cookie. She loved the stuff, and I worried that it might lead her to stronger things.

I could see that she was moodier now, and I didn't care for that side of her personality, but when she was high, she was a ton of fun, and besides, who was I to tell someone how to live their life.

"Hey, we got a stripper tonight. I hear she's no Lili St. Cyr, but we do what we can," Vinny said and laughed. He was always cracking himself up. I shook my head and went on to my station to quickly fill my cigarette box. I needed to get out to the floor nothing but fast. Cookie had a routine that cut her packing time in half . . . but then she was doing a lot of things faster these days . . . talking, walking, etc. . . . But it was the annoying twitch she'd developed that bothered me the most.

About that time, I heard a commotion coming from the office, and a tall, lanky blonde came running out, with the boss hot on her heels.

"And stay out!" he called, and then, glancing at me he smoothed back his thick hair. I caught his eyes looking me over from head to toe, and then, with a quick side glance to his bodyguard, who stood at the door, he snapped his finger and pointed at me, signaling the brute to manhandle me into the office. I figured I was about to be fired for sure. Nothing like being caught late when the boss was in a bad mood, I thought to myself.

"You dance?" he asked.

"Sure, but—"

"Fine," he snapped, tossing a skimpy sequin outfit at me. "Tonight, on the stage, you'll dance in that."

"What?" I gawked. He didn't answer me, but instead, I was manhandled out of the office, past Cookie, who I knew wondered what mess I had gotten myself into now, and on into Ms. St. Cyr's old dressing room.

"And hurry up!" the thug barked, slamming the door.

Standing in front of the mirror, looking down at my thin frame, I had to wonder what in the heck that man was thinking.

The lights dimmed after the MC announced me as the new discovery . . . E! I figured he must have asked Cookie what my name was and that was the answer he got. I stumbled onto the stage, dragging the dress, which was way too long for me, stuffed and padded and ready to dance for an audience of horny men all hoping to get a peep show of a professional quality. The music started, and I stood like a deer in the headlights until the first boo came. Looking around, nearly panicked, I spied Cookie and Vinny flanking the stage behind the curtain. Cookie began to move to the music, instructing me to follow her lead, which I did. Like I said, the girl was good, and soon the men were hooting and hollering and Vinny was drooling. And, I managed to do it all without showing an inch of my privacy.

It didn't take long to get into the act, and soon I didn't need Cookie to shadow from step to step. By the end of the week, I had developed a whole routine. I had heard of a dancer who used fans, and so I incorporated them into my act as well, also finding that something a bit more fitted helped. My legs weren't bad, and so I showed them, but not having much on top, I hid that area as much as possible behind the fans, only giving them the bare cheeks of my backside to see. I knew I had plenty of that to share, as I took after my aunt Rebecca in that department. The older I got, the more I saw the resemblance in that area.

The money was good, and soon Cookie and I moved into a nice little apartment not far off the strip. She sold cigarettes, smoked pot, and longed to be on the stage, and I was on the stage, wishing in a way I was still selling cigarettes. But it was just another example of how my life went.

Again, I dyed my hair blond, and this time I came out a flaming carrottop. The boss loved it, and so did Vinny.

One night after the show, Vinny finally made a move on his emotions. He asked me out. I agreed. He was sweet and awkward, as if he hadn't been on a real date before.

"Order whatever ya want," he said. "You're just a little girl. I'm sure you don't eat much." He laughed loudly.

"Yeah, you'd think that," I told him, looking over the menu, rubbing my empty belly. I was going to show him how *little* girls ate. . . .

Vinny and I laughed and talked for a long time after the shock of my eating abilities wore off. But then he looked at his watch as if he had to get back.

"You gotta get back?" I asked.

"The boss don't like it when I'm not there at closing."

"There's a closing?"

"Well, when the money comes through. I'm there to watch over things . . . you know, in case there's trouble."

"Oh, then what do you do?"

Vinny chuckled and then, as if realizing I truly wanted an answer, he smiled slyly. "I take care of it," he answered.

The light came on, and I gasped slightly. "Oh, I get it," I said, chuckling nervously. "You ever have to *fix* things?"

"You ask a lot of questions."

"Just curious."

"You know what they say about curiosity," he warned.

"Yes, I do and I'm sorry."

"Don't be sorry, pixy," he said.

"Pixy, huh. I like that," I flirted.

"Yeah, I want you to like it."

"You got any questions for me?" I asked, wanting to see what might be rolling around in his head.

"Yeah, actually . . . I wanna know why your friend keeps asking me for *stuff.*"

"Stuff?"

"Yeah, stuff . . . ya know. . . . She got some kinda narcotic problem? Because if she does, the boss is gonna have to let her go. I've been covering for the botha ya because . . . well, because I like you. But your friend, I'm not so sure about her."

"Cookie is okay. She's just an excited person." I covered for her. I had had a feeling I wasn't the only person noticing the changes in Cookie's mannerisms. I was going to have to talk to her when I got home tonight. Cookie losing her job could be bad for both of us.

"You're a good friend. I can tell that, and I like that in a woman."

"Thank you."

"Let's get outta here."

"And go where?"

"We'll drive for a bit and maybe, like, make out or something," he said, and then laughed, although I was sure he was serious.

We drove for a while, but making out was not in my

plans. I didn't think it was wise to tie work and play together. After explaining that, Vinny had to agree.

In front of my place, Vinny kissed me in the car. He had a tough way about him, but he was a big guy, and I could tell he wasn't trying to rough me up.

"Can I come in?" he asked.

"I think Cookie would get mad."

"Cookie? She's a jealous kitty. I'd keep my eye on her."

"You don't know women very well, Vinny."

"What do you mean by that?"

"You thought I didn't eat much."

He burst into laughter and then hugged me tight before allowing me to get out of the car.

Cookie had waited up, or at least I caught her looking out the window. But when I got inside and started to tell her about the evening, she immediately started yawning and acting tired.

Maybe Vinny was right.

I went out with Vinny a few more times, and it seemed the closer he and I got, the more Cookie started getting in his face. One night I could have even sworn I saw her flirting with Vinny near the hatcheck area. When she saw me, she walked off quickly, without even saying hello to me or good-bye to him. Even he looked puzzled. But then, that wasn't hard for Vinny.

At dinner, he told how she was practically throwing herself at him. "Yeah, if I wasn't a simple, one-sighted man, I'da went for it," he admitted. "She's got a monkey on her back . . . I'm telling you."

"One-sighted?" I asked, ignoring the warning about Cookie's growing drug problem. I lived with her; I already knew about it. He winked at me.

"You know I'm crazy about you, kid," he admitted. "You got me one-sighted seeing only you. I'm hoping one of these days you'll let me show you just how much."

"You've shown me, Vinny, and you've been nothing but a gentleman about it, too. You're a great guy."

He blushed slightly.

Chapter 20

"You know Vinny is a criminal, don't you? You know he's got connections with some very scary people, E?" Cookie asked me while watching me apply my heavy make-up. I glanced at her over my shoulder.

"As long as he's not a Klansman, I can handle whatever connections he's got," I joked. Cookie looked at me cockeyed. I realized she had no idea why I had said that. "Anyway, it's no big deal. I like him. We're friends."

"I'm just saying be careful, E. I hear things," Cookie explained.

"Like what?"

"I just hear stuff . . . and frankly, I'm thinking about quitting."

"And finding a job where?" I asked her. My hands were on my hips now, and I showed my irritation. Every time something got easy, there was always somebody throwing a wrench in the deal. "If you quit, it's gonna mess up everything."

"For who?" Cookie asked. "You got it made in the shade. Me? I'm a cigarette girl." Her words exposed her jealousy. I had wondered how long it would take to come out.

"Cookie, I didn't ask to dance on stage."

"But you didn't turn the job down, either, now did you?"

"I didn't see you complaining when I put that turkey on the table for Thanksgiving!" I snapped. "How ungrateful."

"Grateful! You want me to be grateful to you? You're nothing to me . . . you're nothing to anybody. I know the truth about you, and with one word to Vinny, I could make all this stop!" she screamed.

"What are you talking about?"

"The letters . . . the letters to your colored cousin!" she screamed.

"You've been through my things? You're gonna stand there looking like a skeleton, drugged out of your mind, and tell me some shit like that and expect me to be scared! No, I'm just angry."

"Well, add this to your *angry* . . . Where do you think I've been getting my drugs?" Cookie, caught up in her confessions, now stepped back to regroup, but it was too late. I was on her, and we were immediately engrossed in a full on altercation. I slapped her hard across the face. I was angry. I knew what she was doing, and it made me sick.

Showing me how she felt about me dating Vinny really wasn't worth all this trouble Cookie was going through. Vinny and I were friends, and I intended to keep it that way. If she was trying to take something from me, she was barking up the wrong tree, as Vinny wasn't mine to take, but what hurt was the way she was going about things . . . behind my back, if in fact she had used Vinny to supply her drugs.

Vinny rang the bell, but we didn't hear him due to all the cursing and fighting, so he opened the door and let himself in. "Hey, what gives!" he yelped, pulling us apart.

"She's a nigger!" Cookie screamed, pointing at me angrily, wiping her blood from her nose.

"What the hell are you talking about, Cookie? You're nuts. E here ain't colored. You're color-blind," he said, laughing at his own joke.

"No, and I can prove it!" she threatened. Vinny looked at her and then at me and then back at her, while standing between us.

"Is this true, E?" he asked.

Now was my chance. I could end this lie once and for all. I could admit to being black and take whatever came with that fact.

"Tell him!" Cookie screamed. "And she's queer!" Cookie added.

I realized then, she knew about Sade, too. My hand covered my mouth in horror and mortification. I wanted to die right then and there, but instead, I ran. I grabbed my purse and car keys and ran from the apartment out to my car. Another person had turned the tables on my life and left me with the empty plate sitting in front of me.

Sure, I could have stood and gone round and round with her . . . and him, for that matter. I could have confronted him about what she had told me about him giving her drugs, but still, in the end, it would have come down to my race being the most important issue.

Good riddance to both of them, I thought to myself. Thank goodness, I had been smart enough to keep my bank account separate from Cookie's. I would have been sunk without the twelve hundred dollars I had stashed away. And, trust me when I say that in 1958 twelve hundred bucks went a long way.

The desert is a lonely place at night, especially when one doesn't know where one is going . . . and that person would be me.

Chapter 21

I'd managed to make it to California, where I landed a job at the local library. I was exhausted all the time. Maybe it was all mental, but it didn't matter. Some days I didn't feel as though I could go on. Loneliness was the worst of it all, I think. I was so very lonely.

I spent most of my time at the library, even after my shifts, and even then, I would take home armfuls of books to read. I didn't care how people viewed me, as I realized now, I *was* weird. The shoe fit well, and so I wore it. My car finally died, and so I traded four wheels for two. I didn't speak to people much outside of the library, and when home, I never went outside nor talked with my neighbors. I'd grown a little paranoid, I guess, as I figured everyone was my enemy, just waiting for the right time to turn on me and cause me problems.

I was angry deep inside as it had been years since I'd left Noah and the safety of his arms. For years now, I had been left to endure all this, and still he had not arrived to gather me up. He hadn't specified that I was to sit in one place and wait, and so I assumed that he had the power to find me anywhere. However, apparently, I was wrong. I wrote Josie every day and Molly, too, but had yet to hear back from either of them. Maybe they both hated me and rightly so. What had I done but betray them both. I had betrayed Molly by not staying white enough, for if I had, I would not have tried to stand with the Negros against the Klan. I wouldn't have used Denny Johnson but, instead, would have married him and saved Molly a lot of trouble. I had betrayed Josie by not returning to my blackness soon enough, for if I had, she would not have to endure alone all the horrors of being in the Deep South during the violent onset of the civil rights movement.

I prayed to God through the ears of my mother, begging for the answer and the direction in which my next step should go. *Stand still, do nothing, wait for Noah . . .* was a hum that was constant, but, of course, I just swatted at the sound of it, the way one would swat at a fat, buzzing fly too close to the ear.

Taking a long, manly size drag from my cigarette, I mashed it out in the ashtray that sat on the stoop of my building on my way in. It had been a particularly long week, and I was glad it was over. I picked up my copy of the newspaper, turning to my favorite editorial section. I had written the editor many times about my views on the possibility of space travel. Again, I looked for my letter to be published, but it was not. I supposed it was beyond the scope of the readers—especially since I would always, in the end, mention how interested I was in living on the moon one day.

"Don't you know the surgeon general is saying that smoking is bad for you?" I heard from behind me.

I spun around, ready to smart off, but was left speechless when, instead of a nosey neighbor, I saw standing there a handsome, fully uniformed, grown-up, and to die for—did I mention that he was drop dead gorgeous—Keith Mitchell.

I thought I would faint. I squealed; I jumped up and down, dropping my mail while I did a jig. I acted nowhere like the lady everyone around me figured I was as he lifted me from the ground in a bear hug to beat all bear hugs.

What a wave of déjà vu overcame me as I looked into the face of what had become my past.

"Wow, have you changed," he said to me from behind his wide grin. There was no way to quickly sum up what all had changed since leaving Minnesota. Then again, by the looks of Keith, he'd done some changing, too. Perhaps it was the war and the threat of active duty always hanging over our heads that had grown him up so fast, but he was a man now, just as I was a woman. I couldn't help but wonder about Peachy and Jerry. With them, we would have been a gang again. How I missed having friends . . . real friends.

Chapter 22

"I almost didn't believe it was you, sugar," Keith said, playfully grabbing a handful of my flaming red hair. I had held on to the color as it really did look pretty good on me. I knew I looked very different now, and I was actually surprised that he had recognized me at all. I took off my jacket and laid it over the back of the sofa.

"I still can't believe it's you!" I told him, wondering how in the world he had found me.

"Well, believe it or not, it's just short of a miracle. I'm stationed here. And me and a couple of guys were wandering around through town, and, well, I saw you in the library. I didn't want to believe it at first, until I asked the other lady your name. She said, 'Emily' and I knew . . ."

"Yeah, I sort of changed my name a little bit, but what's the crime in that, right?"

"Exactly . . . where's the crime, right?"

The moment between us lasted longer than was comfortable, and so I slowly moved out of the space I was in.

"Are you hungry? I mean, I don't have much food, but I . . ."

"No, actually, I came by to see if you wanted to go out with me," he said.

"Oh, course . . . of course, I do. I never eat out . . . and nobody ever comes over, either."

"You don't get company?"

"I don't have many friends." I chuckled. "I don't have any friends," I confessed.

"That's no way to live, Emmy," he said, catching my eyes in his gaze. My heart fluttered. "I guess I have to change that."

"You?"

"I've always liked you, Emmy . . . Emily." He chuckled.

Is Keith the one? I asked my mother silently. Was it to be a white man that made me whole . . . completed me? Was it to be a white man that made all this make sense? Had he come to claim me in Noah's stead?

I was so confused by my feelings . . . my heart tussling with my mind, Keith's lips on mine, his strong arms holding me tight.

I undressed quickly and climbed into bed beside him, my shyness at bay only due to familiarity. Keith's touch was soft and gentle, soothing and ever so appreciated. I lavished in his kisses and allowed him full exploration of my body. I couldn't believe how he wanted me . . . black as I was. I gasped and shook while giving in to the sensations he caused to come up in me. Although they were not nearly as intense as the ones I had only in my memory from the day in Noah's room, they would do for now. They soothed for now. I held him tight, noticing only a slight difference in our skin tones. It wasn't like the day I held Noah . . . Black and white, we were, odd and maybe even mismatched.

Holding Keith felt natural, or maybe I just wanted to feel that way. All I knew was that I had prayed and Keith had come. . . .

We reminisced about many things. Trudy, who I still referred to as Peachy, had married and had two children. Jerry had become a pilot in the air force and was somewhere overseas now. And many of our other mutual friends had stayed in Wisconsin, living simple lives . . . lives the two of us could only envy now.

After our lovemaking, we showered, dressed, and went down to the cafe that was near my place.

"I can't believe you are in the military," I said, taking a large bite from my plate.

He looked around nervously. "For now," he said, sounding mysterious.

"For now." I took on the same tone of mystery.

"I know how you used to feel about political things. I mean, I don't know if you are still on that level, but for me . . ."

"Yes, I know I was a little headstrong in that area, but I've . . ." I giggled, thinking about my viewpoints on certain matters. I didn't want to tell him that I still had many of the same views. Why start trouble with a military man? Why start trouble with the man who had come to save me?

"I could take or leave this country . . . and I'm planning to leave it."

"Pardon me?" I choked. My head spun a little.

"Me and a couple of friends are headed to Canada as soon as we can find a way there."

"Keith, no. . . . You're gonna desert?" I whispered. He shushed me, leaning in close. If we didn't look conspicuous before, we did now, with our heads together. My heart was pounding.

"Yeah, I am," he confessed. "And seeing you, Emmy, finding you here, just made me realize how easily it could work. I mean, look at how long you've been on the lam, and if you weren't so damn pretty, I wouldn't have even recognized you."

"On the lam?"

"Yeah . . . the Griffith thing. You know, they are still looking for you."

"Me? Why? I didn't kill Mr. Griffith."

"That's not what I hear. I hear you and Greta conspired and planned the whole thing. My father is a lawyer, remember. He told me the whole story." Keith paused and looked around. "The whole story," he added slyly. I knew exactly what he meant now, and I sat back in my seat, looking around.

I often dashed into this small cafe on my way home from work and took my dinner home in a box. It was cozy and friendly, but I had never eaten here. However, I had planned to start dining in. Suddenly, I realized that was never going to happen; my life was about to change—again.

"What do you want from me?" I asked, cutting to the chase.

"Nothing, Emmy," Keith answered, sounding a bit surprised at my question.

"Come on, Keith. Everybody wants something," I answered coldly. "You get me to bed, take my mind for a minute, catch me off guard . . . God, I need a cigarette," I growled, digging into my purse. Keith grabbed my shaking hands.

"Haven't you ever just felt like something just happened because it was supposed to?" he said then. "Haven't you ever felt like something was just meant to be?"

"No," I lied.

"Well, I did. And ever since I met you, I realized you were different. You weren't like the other girls . . . like Trudy. You were always smarter and, well . . . different.

Then, when my dad told me the truth about you, I realized why. You are different. This afternoon with you . . . was . . . different, Emmy," he said, sounding a little softer now. I knew he meant it . . . at least that part. It had been different, for me too . . . considering it had only been the second time in my life I'd made love to anyone.

"What did your dad tell you about me?"

"What do you think?" Keith answered. I sighed heavily. I knew I would lose my job when they found out they had hired a Negro. I would lose my apartment, too. Times were changing, but not enough to where I could come out of hiding without repercussions, and besides, why would I? Although lonely, I had gotten by rather well over the last year or so.

"Jeeeze, Keith, I just love being pulled over a barrel this way."

"Well, you're the criminal, not me. At least not yet." He snickered.

"So you're figuring to run alongside me, with me as a shield."

"Murder is a much bigger crime than desertion, trust me."

"When did you think of all this?"

"The moment I saw you," he confessed. "Come on, Emmy, you and me . . . against the world. What do you say? Come to Canada with me?"

"Chain of Fools." It would be years before Aretha Franklin would sing the song that best described my time with Keith. If only I had had her soulful voice singing those words to me right then, I might have realized what was going on a lot sooner. I would never have packed my bags and left with Keith like I did. But there were only crooners singing about the wonders of love and togetherness during that time; there was only bad news about war and racial upheavals in one place after another in the news. Why would I give up on what I thought was the possibility of love and acceptance to be part of all the negativity going on around me? Why would I give up on having a strong man to hold me to be independent and alone again? I know it seemed like such a minor thing, Keith and I not being married, considering all the other illegalities we were dealing with—him being a deserter and me being on the lam for murder. However, I had to figure that the reason we weren't married was because it would be interracial, and we really didn't need that extra crime on our heads.

A commune in Venice Beach was nowhere near the Canadian border, but that was where we settled in. The house was filled with him and me, along with a few of his comrades who had hidden from active duty months before. Why we all figured that living so close to a navel base, we would not be noticed was puzzling sometimes.

It didn't take long before nearly everyone had moved on. It was a relief to me. Sharing that small place with three other women, let alone their raggedy boyfriends, wrecked my nerves.

Despite our liberal lifestyle, we still needed money, and there was no way Keith could get a regular job, so he worked odd jobs, which kept him away from home a lot. I hated being home with Popeye, who was the most obnoxious of his friends, and Popeye's girlfriend, Judy, so when he wasn't there, I would often find myself at the library, and that's where I met Theo Fairbanks. Of course, it would take another turn of events before we would meet up again, but it was in that library that day, when our hands touched while reaching for the same criminal law book, that I noticed him. I wasn't sure he noticed me, but then again, I wasn't very noticeable. Wearing clothes that we got from wherever we could find them, I'm sure I looked less than impressive. My hair had outgrown its color, but Keith had refused to let me cut it, so I'm sure I looked like some kind of gypsy or circus freak. But Theo was nice and handed me the book, stating that it looked as if I could use it more than he. I figured him for a graduate student and just assumed he was there studying. He said he was going to be a civil rights attorney and had a test in a few days, so I just put two and three together. As for me, I was reading up on my position in the Griffith case. I wanted to know if I was truly innocent of murder, just in case we all ended up in jail before this was all said and done. Harboring fugitives was one thing, but murder was quite another.

Finally, after running into him three days in a row, I asked Theo about the Griffith case, hypothetically, of course, and it was just as I thought. Keith had lied. There was no way the police were still hunting for me. Greta Griffith had confessed and had been convicted, and that was all they needed to close the case. She had been the one behind the trigger. Theo even helped me find the newspaper articles that stated just that fact, never asking me why I wanted to know about this particular case. I felt appreciative, and it was a natural gesture for me to help him find the information he was there looking for. Besides, I was fascinated in the subject of the civil rights movement, which was growing in the South. It was after several hours that I realized it was past time to get back to the house.

"It's pretty late. Do you want to go to dinner?" he asked me.

"No, I . . ." I paused, glancing around, hoping that Keith would not pull up in the truck to pick me up as he sometimes did when I was out too late. "But I'll be here tomorrow," I told him, hoping that meant he would be also. He simply smiled and smoothed back his hair.

"Well, perhaps we'll run into each other again sometime," he said, and then turning back to me after he had started to walk away, he held up his notepad and added, "And thanks again for the help."

"Anytime . . . it's the subject I know best," I called out.

"I see," he replied.

When I got back to the house, it was in an uproar, as usual. All everyone did was fight. It was getting ridiculous, and I wished Keith and I could move, but he insisted that we needed to all stay together, something about being partners in crime. I didn't think being Negro was such a big offense; however, I was sure he meant my involvement in the incident surrounding Mr. Griffith.

"You know, that happened such a long time ago, I'm sure it's forgotten," I said that night toward Keith's back. I knew he wasn't asleep, as my house mates had argued loudly for the last hour and a half . . . who could sleep?

"How many times do I have to tell you, there is no statute of limitations on murder?" he grumbled.

"But, surely, we could move and . . ."

He turned back to me; I could see his eyes glowing in the darkness. "What have I said about that? We can't leave Popeye and Judy. . . . They need us."

"Why? I mean, they seem to be able to fight well enough on their own," I pointed out, aiming my words at the thin wall that separated us. "Why are they together, anyway? . . . What does Popeye have on Judy that keeps her trapped?"

I didn't realize how my words sounded, but they caused Keith to rise up on one elbow. "Is that how you feel? Trapped with me?"

I touched his chest. "I didn't mean that."

"Sure, you did. You said it and you meant it."

"Keith, let's not fight. It's not worth a fight . . . it was a dumb statement, and I'm sorry I said it."

I kissed him, and it seemed to calm him down a bit, as he began to rub my thigh and stomach, as he often did before deciding if we would make love. Over the last few months, our money had been tight, and so our birth control methods were lazy at best. It was such an inconvenience these days trying to find the money for rubbers, so he was using the pull-out method, which was not all that reliable. I had been thinking a lot about going to see a doctor. I'd been hearing about a new contraceptive they simply called the pill. It was still in experimental stages, but it would be worth a try. It seemed as though Keith was totally fine with the idea of being with a black woman, but having a black child . . . well, I just wasn't so sure. He'd made comments about black people, comments that sometimes surprised me, considering I was black. It was as if he sometimes forgot that fact . . . or that he didn't know. But I was sure he did. He all but told me he did, right? But sometimes it seemed as if he didn't.

Spreading my legs, I allowed Keith to enter me without a condom. I could tell by the way he went for it, he had no intention of pulling out. We had made love the night before this way, as if we didn't have a care in the world. Keith always said such pretty things about me while making love to me, and I couldn't resist the sound of his voice in my ear. When we finished, he lay there on me for a while, stroking my hair and kissing my face.

"Marry me, Emmy," he said.

"Really? You want us to get married?"

"Of course, I do . . . why wouldn't I?"

"Well, I figured you didn't want any other troubles."

Keith laughed. "How could being married cause troubles? If anything, it's a good thing . . . you can't testify against me in court." He laughed.

"Why would you go to court?" I asked. He shushed me with a kiss.

"I'm just saying, if it ever came up about the murder, I would be able to stand by you is all. That's what I meant to say," he corrected.

"Well, if I marry you, can I have a baby?" I asked.

"Sure, sugar, you can have all the babies you want . . ." he agreed.

"You're not scared of how they'll come out?"

"They'll come out of where I'm in right now," he joked. I chuckled, too.

"No, silly . . . they could come out looking like my mother."

"Well, its better than them coming out looking like Greta Griffith . . . she was one ugly woman. When my father told me the truth about your being adopted, I was actually relieved. I mean, I know it was hard on you to keep that secret, but it's really okay . . . considering. And I know you didn't have nothing to do with killing the old man. I know that."

"Being adopted? Is that all your father told you about me?" I asked, trying to keep the conversation focused, trying not to panic.

"What else was there to tell?" he asked, sounding sincere.

I lay there under him, still and silent. I was so still, it was as if I could feel myself becoming pregnant at that very moment.

"Nothing," I lied.

Chapter 23

I went back to the library every day for weeks, looking for Theo Fairbanks, but he never showed up. What was I thinking, trying to see him, anyway? I had bigger issues. I was pregnant. I was black. And Keith was ignorant of both of those facts.

No money for even a stamp, I tried to deal with my thoughts alone. I tried to figure out where I was in the scheme of time and where I was supposed to go next.

I could marry Keith, have the baby, and hope for the best. Or I could marry Keith, have my black baby, and he could kill me dead. Abortion was illegal. I knew that, but in this case, I felt it was the better of two evils.

About that time while sitting outside the library, I saw Judy. It was unusual to see her wandering around alone, and so I called out to her. She looked around, and then seeing me, she came to where I was.

"What are you doing here?" she asked me. "Popeye sent you to find me or something?"

"No, why would he do that?"

"Because he doesn't like me out alone."

"You sound like his pet."

She looked away and then back at me. "I feel like I am."

"Well, you're not. You are in control of your own destiny. Even if you make a mistake, claim it and get through it," I said, trying to sound like the big sister type.

"I'm only fourteen. It's not that easy," Judy confessed. I about passed out.

"Fourteen!"

Well, no wonder we lived the way we did. Here we were, two deserters, a black woman, and a minor . . . weren't we a motley crew.

"Popeye could go to jail being with me," she whispered.

"He could go to jail for a lot of things," I agreed. I suddenly needed a cigarette. I hadn't been able to afford my habit and, therefore, was forced to quit, but today I was willing to steal one.

"Why are you so upset about me and Popeye? I didn't think you cared about stuff like that."

"Like what?"

"Couples' stuff. I mean, the way you shared Keith with those other two girls in the house. I didn't figure you—"

"What?"

"Yeah, sharing . . . That's what Popeye called it, anyway. I was gonna do it with him, but Popeye didn't want me to."

That night I had an earful for Keith when he got home. I was angry, and he was going to hear about it. How dare he share what was mine with those other women . . . and right under my nose! I was fuming, and I would be damned if I was going to sit there and let that child be abused by a twenty-something-year-old man. I was gonna pop from all the anger I felt inside. I knew Popeye was even older than Keith was and had no business with someone like Judy.

"It's disgusting!" I yelped.

"Keep your voice down, Emmy. That's why I didn't want to tell you anything, and about Marybeth and Sinclair . . . It was just one or two times we did that. I never wanted you to find out. I knew you would react this way," Keith said, attempting to shush me—again.

"And this . . . *be quiet, Emma,* stuff is bullshit. I'm tired of it," I screamed. My Texan drawl was strong tonight. I could hear the Molly in me coming out.

"What are you saying? You don't want to obey me anymore?"

"Obey you? Is that what you think we got going here? . . . A little master . . . slave thing going on?"

"Now why would you say that? I would never treat you like some nigger woman . . . I would never treat you that low."

"Low?" I went on. There was no stopping me now, oh, but how I wished my mother had asked an angel to do the honors. "So you think being some nigger woman would make me low?" I went on.

"Em, you are talking crazy now. How did we even get on this subject?"

"We were never far from it," I snapped.

"I am not following you. Try speaking slower . . . I know you can make yourself understood if you just try."

"Well, how about I try spelling it out? . . . I am a Negro. There! I said it. I'm black! As black as they come, and this baby inside me is black, too. Ha! I guess your father left out some things in his report! I thought you knew. I thought maybe Peachy had told you, but, no, she was a better friend than I gave her credit for. . . ."

"Emma, what did you just say?" Keith asked. His voice was low and stiff sounding, intimidating, but I was hot and huffed and didn't know what all I had just said. I just knew I had said too much. I backed away from him. His eyes were glassed over, as if he'd been hit by a brick or maybe by the past.

"Trudy knew?" said Keith.

"I told her . . . or she figured it out, I can't remember."

"She told me once you wanted to go to some colored church, but we thought it was just for kicks. I. . . . I didn't know you . . ." I could see Keith thinking back, wondering when and how he'd missed the information.

"Yes, Keith, and that's why the Griffiths adopted me from my mother. My mother wanted me to have a better life . . . a life of freedom. Not one oppressed and . . ." I stepped toward him, hoping to touch him, but he stepped back.

"And now you're pregnant?" he said, twisting his face up, as if the realization of who or, better yet, what he'd been sharing his bed with was hitting him as well. It was a double whammy and more than his little mind could handle, I could tell.

"Yes, Keith, I'm pregnant with your baby," I told him.

He was whirling from the shock of it all. I could tell by the look on his face. And when Popeye entered the room, Keith couldn't keep it all in. "We gotta dump these chicks," he said. Popeye looked at me and then back at Keith.

"Okay," was all Popeye said, as if he'd been ready the whole time for the signal to split.

"Dump? You're just gonna leave me now?" I asked.

"You got that right. You and that tar baby in your belly . . . I'm done," Keith said, pushing past me and on to our bedroom. I followed.

"Keith, you can't just abandon me like this."

"Oh, you'll be fine. From what I've seen, your people are quite resilient," he said sarcastically. I slapped him.

At the sound of my hand striking his cheek the moment became abruptly silent. I knew he wanted to hit me back, but for some reason, he didn't. Maybe because it would have been just too easy, or maybe it was the only moment of strength Keith had ever shown in his life.

"Keith, please!" I begged, before catching my pride. I followed him back to the living room. "What about Judy, Popeye? You can't just leave her alone. She's a child."

"You baby-sit for a while," Popeye said, thinking his comment funny. He'd packed his things in a matter of minutes and had his duffle bag already on his shoulders. It was as if he'd been waiting for just this moment.

"You two are cowards. You ran from the war, and now you are running from girls! You used me Keith. I was never in any trouble. You used me to stay free," I added, trying to say as many mean things as I could think of.

"And you used me to feel white . . . and that didn't work out, either, huh," replied Keith.

"What does that mean?" Popeye asked. Keith just raised his hand in surrender.

"I'll tell you all about it later, Pop," he said, fanning Popeye toward the front door. "Stay out of jail, beautiful . . ." He shook his head as if realizing what he'd called me. "And you are beautiful," he whispered.

When Judy came home, I told her what had occurred. She was furious with me for ruining her relationship. It took hours for her to see how wrong it all was being with Popeye.

"Where do your parents live?" I asked her later that night, after she had calmed down a little.

"San Leandro. I'm so far from home," she cried. "They probably think I'm dead."

"Well, now you can go home, and they can be happy again."

"I can't go home."

"Why, sweetie?"

"Because I'm not who I was when I left."

I laughed, thinking of the irony of her statement. "Nobody is."

I hugged her tight just before her bus pulled off. I had worked all week at a laundromat to get the money together for her ticket. It left me with about thirty dollars, and with that, I went in search of a woman who would abort my baby.

"You white gals always coming out our way when you need something done," the dark-skinned woman said, sounding grouchy and irritable. "Who's the daddy? Some colored boy?" she asked.

"I don't think that matters," I answered, hoping that I didn't sound rude. But I could tell by her huff that my comment hit her wrong.

"Climb up here on this table," she barked.

"Don't you need to get prepared or something?" I asked. I had no idea that darkness was the only preparation she needed. I was scared, to say the least.

"I'm as prepared as you are," she answered. "Now get up here, and open ya legs real wide fa me," she instructed. "That should come easy," she joked, popping her chewing gum.

"Please stop . . . please," I begged, feeling my eyes burning as I fought back tears.

"Why you getting this done if you love the man?" she asked, thinking she saw something hiding behind my tears.

"I don't love him. Not really . . . I thought . . ." I paused. "I thought he loved me, though," I told her.

The pain was excruciating, and I thought she had killed me when I felt the gush of blood leaving me. It had taken all of ten minutes.

"That's it," she said, helping me back up to a sitting position.

"That's all?" I asked, barely holding on to my faculties. I felt instantly weak.

"Well, except my money." She grinned, exposing her gold tooth. I reached in my bra and handed her the thirty dollars. "Get up now so I can take this table-cloth off here and throw it out."

I remember trying to stand and that was all.

When I woke up, I was in a clean hospital bed. I looked around at the unfamiliar surroundings. There were a few other beds in the room, with sleeping women. I wondered if I was in jail.

"Where am I?" I called out. "Help me!" I called out louder, realizing I was strapped to the bed.

The nurse scurried in. "Oh, my, you're awake. You've been unconscious for a while. I'll have to get the doctor right away," she said, scurrying back out.

I was terrified and lay quietly when the doctor came in and pulled the curtain closed around the bed I was in, then examined me. I was tender, and everywhere he touched hurt.

"We've given you a D & C. You've healed nicely, Mrs.?"

"Sampson," I answered, quickly trying to take in all that was happening. Whatever the doctor had done to me, it was going to go over better if I was a Mrs. That I could tell right away.

"Ahh, Mrs. Sampson. Yes, it is a pity you've lost the baby, but you're a healthy woman, and I'm sure you and your husband can try again. Think of it as nature's way of fixing things," he said.

"I lost my baby?" I asked, trying to sound surprised.

He looked at the nurse. "Why, yes. Your housekeeper brought you in, said you were bleeding and had passed out. Don't you remember?"

"No, I . . . I mean, yes. My housekeeper?" I asked, thinking of the last woman I'd seen before losing consciousness. The gold-toothed woman who looked more like a blues singer in some smoky bar. I couldn't imagine her cleaning anyone's home. She was too prideful and mean. But then again . . . she hadn't let me die, which apparently would have been easy to do.

"We didn't find any identification on you. Your housekeeper said she didn't have time to gather anything up, but then again, sometimes good help is so hard to find," he went on, before pulling the curtain away.

"Why am I strapped down?"

"Well, you've been in a coma for several hours, and it was for your safety," he said, instructing the nurse to untie me. "And, Mrs. Sampson, we're sorry about this not being a private room, but as I said, we didn't have any identification. I'm sure you could afford a private room, but . . ."

"No, I'm fine with the room. When can I go home?" I asked.

"We'd like to call your husband. We'll need him to sign some insurance papers, anyway. How does that sound? We'll call him to come pick you up and take care of payment." I did not have a clue who they might call, as Noah Sampson, last I knew, didn't have a phone.

"No! No . . . I hadn't told him I was pregnant. It was going to be a surprise. He'd be devastated if he were to find out this way. Please can you send the bill to my home . . . or, better yet, to my sister's home?" I lied.

They looked at each other. "I'm sure billing can work something out," the nurse finally answered.

"You don't think he's missed you?" the doctor finally asked.

"No, you see . . ." I thought quickly now. "He's been out of town on business. He won't be home until next week. He's a very important lawyer and . . ."

"I understand," the doctor jumped in, patting my arm. "I totally understand. We'll get the papers drawn up, and perhaps you can go home in the morning. Will that be okay?"

I settled back in the bed, figuring that would be plenty of time to sneak outta this place. "Yes, that will be fine."

It was after the nurse's last rounds that I made my escape. My clothes were missing, and so I took those that belonged to the woman who lay comatose in the bed across from me. She hadn't been awake all day, and so I knew she wouldn't be needing them anytime soon.

Once outside, I attempted to walk without limping or otherwise showing pain, greeting all the nurses and other medical staff coming and going as if I had been there visiting someone ill, instead of being quite ill myself.

I didn't know where I was headed, but I knew getting away from that hospital was a start.

The boulevard was a jumping spot that night. And I walked as long as I could, before coming upon a cheap-looking hotel. I had no money but needed some sleep bad. There was a bench out front of the office, and so I laid my head down on it and was out like a light.

The next morning I felt better. A little stiff, but better. Surprisingly enough, I hadn't been taken to jail. It was a miracle actually as the night before the area had been hopping with cops.

Needless to say, Noah was on my mind. I had used his name to get out of the hospital and had put a baby on him that he had had no part in making. For that, I felt ashamed, as I knew there would be no way in hell I would have killed Noah's baby. I swore then to myself and all the invisible folks listening that I would never have another child by a man I didn't love.

I had managed to have an illegal abortion and live. Maybe my mother had asked for mercy on my behalf. Maybe she had pointed out to the good Lord how hard I had tried this time to get myself out of trouble—backassward as my efforts might have been.

I must have wandered for hours before coming upon a church. I thought about going in. It was a Catholic church, and I knew there would be a confessional booth there. Although I wasn't Catholic, I wanted to confess. I wanted to tell my sins to whoever would listen, but noting the finely dressed people coming and going, I opted against it.

Maybe I would find a Baptist church and pray there. But then, remembering the Bickel incident, I realized that might not work out, either. I wandered on. Finally, out of energy, hope, and ideas, I flopped down on the grass of the UCLA campus. It was cool under me. The birds sang and the sky sparkled. It was a beautiful day.

Suddenly, I saw him . . . Theo Fairbanks. I scrambled to my feet, and with all the strength I had left, I made my way over to him, stopping a little distance from him so as not to embarrass him, as he was with his colleagues, and I knew I must have looked a fright. He, on the other hand, was looking fresh and happy, walking with his colleagues laughing and talking.

No doubt feeling my stare, he glanced my way, and then, with a sudden realization of who I was, he bid his friends good-bye and walked over to me. "Well, hello," he greeted me, sounding chipper and perky. I smiled and smoothed down my hair and ill-fitting clothing. "If it isn't my bohemian friend."

"Yes . . . 'tis I." I chuckled, realizing only now what he thought of me. "You remember me?" I asked, trying to control my breathing. I was hungry and nearly out of breath from rushing over to him.

"Of course, I remember you. A man doesn't meet a beautiful woman like you and quickly forget," he answered flatly. He wasn't shy, and that was good, because I was about to faint and didn't have time to play coy.

"Well, does a man like you ask a beautiful woman like me out for"—I took him by the wrist, turning his watch so that I could see the time, as I had no idea—"an early dinner, perhaps?"

He laughed. "Of course. He'd be a fool not to. And besides, I could use the stimulating conversation." He held out his arm, and I quickly took it . . . more for support than anything.

"By the way, what is your name, beautiful lady?" he asked.

I thought about it for a moment. "What do you want it to be?"

He laughed. "Let me think about that."

One dinner led to many as Theo pretended not to notice my destitution, or perhaps he expected it from me. He never asked where I had come from when I met him at the college on our dates. He had no idea

I had been sleeping on the street and bathing at the YWCA, or he didn't care. I wore the same clothes over and over. I could have gotten clothes from the Salvation Army, but why give myself the extra burden of clothes to wash or to carry around with me? That is, until he decided to take our relationship to the next level.

"I want you to meet some of my friends, Emma," he said, cutting his steak. I, too, was heartily enjoying my meal. Theo wasn't cheap when it came to feeding me. I could order whatever I wanted, and so I did. Up till now, it all came with no strings attached. Theo seemed to truly enjoy my companionship. I know I enjoyed his. He fed me and stimulated my thinking, all without pressure to do anything I didn't want to do. Now if only he would bed me down, I would have it made. These weeks on the street were wearing on me. I didn't want necessarily to have sex with him—there just hadn't been that kind of attraction—but sleeping in a bed . . . I wanted that bad enough to do it if he wanted me to. But I kept my thoughts to myself. Something told me that Theo didn't need sexual favors to be a gentleman.

"Your friends?" I asked after swallowing hard.

"Yes, I'm having a social, and I thought it would be a perfect time to introduce my colleagues to my girlfriend."

"Girlfriend?"

"Well, yes . . . You are my girlfriend, aren't you?"

"Well, I'm your friend."

"And most definitely a girl . . ." he added, raising an eyebrow. It was a cute facial expression for Theo to make, and it made me giggle. He could be so cute sometimes, without even trying.

"I wondered if you had noticed."

"I notice a lot of things," he said.

"Like what?"

"I notice that you're not one to try to get a man to do what you want by seduction. I notice that you respect my preferences by allowing me to move our relationship along at my pace. I notice that you're homeless, and I would definitely like to help you."

I looked around the restaurant, hoping no one had heard him say those words to me, as I had yet to say them out loud to myself. It was a fact that I was having a hard time with, despite dealing with it every day. There was something about what Molly had said once about a lady never allowing herself to become homeless. I think that is what made this whole situation so wrong to me.

Theo went on. "You're open-minded and, apparently, single and available. . . ."

"You notice a lot," I remarked, sipping my Coca-Cola.

"I notice there is something different about you, and one day I would hope you would tell me what that difference is . . . but for now, it makes you mysterious and, well . . . simply wonderful to be with."

"You make me blush, Theo." I giggled.

"It's Assemblyman Fairbanks. I'm about to run for Congress. I want you by my side."

I was shocked. I'd been so out of the loop, I'd not even read a recent newspaper. Here I was, dating possibly the future president of the United States, and I didn't even know it.

"Congress?"

"The House . . . and then, who knows, perhaps the Senate . . . perhaps . . . the world," he added, bursting into laughter.

I was stunned and could barely chew the bite of food in my mouth. "I can't believe you never told me."

"Well, we all have our secrets . . . I know you have

some." He smiled, touching my hand softly. My eyes went from his hand to his eyes . . . his caring eyes.

A single assemblyman, how could this occur? But then, apparently, Theo was ready to change things, or at least his friends were. He was reaching for the big brass ring, and he needed me. Yes, it was true, I was taking the risk of walking into another situation where I was going to be abused, but I was willing to take that chance with Theo. For some reason, I felt in my heart, he would never hurt me as the others had.

I have to admit that I was a little uncomfortable about having a man pick out and buy my clothes. Especially when we entered the expensive store and all the salesgirls looked at me as if I had just dropped in from planet grunge. I could see the question in their eyes, How did *he* end up with *her*?

Both the women there seemed to know Theo and his mother well, so they were almost forced to be nice to me. So I dug deep, trying to put on my most lady-like ways. I'd found the best rags to wear to that store that day; I'm even trying to remember if I made a special trip to the Salvation Army to pick up a new skirt. But even with those efforts, I must have looked like some waif coming in there with Theo Fairbanks, the most eligible bachelor in politics.

Theo found a comfortable chair and didn't seem to mind at all as the minutes turned to hours. He seemed to thoroughly enjoy watching me go through, literally, a ton of outfits.

I felt pretty and special when he applauded a couple of times, when I came out in a particularly beautiful gown or a well-fitting pair of slacks. I tell you, the man knew how he wanted me to look, and his taste was impeccable. Finally, he decided on purchasing me at least a dozen things, from casual Capri pants to a beautiful, dressy red evening gown. It couldn't have been more enjoyable a shopping spree than if I had gone with my best girlfriend.

When we went to shop for shoes, Theo bought himself a new pair of snakeskin boots. I convinced him they would look wonderful on him. I'd almost talked him into a Stetson, but he was not quite ready for that one.

"So how long did you live in Texas?" he asked me while we strolled Sunset Boulevard. It was where all the starlets shopped, and so I wanted to go there to see who I could catch out in public, but so far we hadn't spied anybody famous. I was hoping that maybe somebody really famous would be out and about . . . but no such luck.

"What makes you think I wasn't born there?"

He laughed.

"So, you think my accent is fake? Well, just so you know, I lived in Dallas for about five years, and it grew on me good. I can't shake it to save my life, but I do suppose it's not quite bone solid."

He chuckled at my explanation. "You're so charming. Who raised you?"

"I thought we covered all this territory before, Theo . . . why suddenly the third degree?"

"Because I want you to do your utmost to be honest with me. Always. Never lie or betray me, and we'll get along just fine."

Was this what romance sounded like? Not in my book. I thought lovers lied. But apparently, Theo liked it straight, and frankly, straight was a lot easier than how I'd been telling it. I was silent for a moment while we strolled a little ways, and then I stopped him and looked him straight in the eye.

"My mother died, and I ended up living with a woman in Texas, who taught me many wonderful things about life. I have to say, she was quite the mother figure for me. Her name is Molly Holsted."

Theo smiled and looked off. I couldn't read his expression and couldn't tell if he believed me or not. "What?" I asked him, trying to get in front of him, which was easy to do, with him weighed down, carrying most of my packages.

"Nothing. I just think you're cute when you . . . uh . . . omit. I really hope you keep that quality."

"Omission is my best feature," I quickly retorted. He chuckled, and we continued to window-shop.

"Good. Because I will be counting on that when you meet my friends and, even more so, when you meet my mother."

"What about your father?"

"My father doesn't care about my friends or me, for that matter, and he isn't as good at lying as you are, so please don't ask him about me or anything for that matter. He's not as charming as you."

"I'm sorry, Theo. I didn't know."

"He's old and cranky, and, well, I have done well just ignoring him for the most part."

"I don't know my father."

"Died before you were born perhaps?" he said. I smiled.

"Exactly," I answered.

Theo had even arranged for me to have my first manicure and pedicure. I felt like Cinderella, and all the ugly things that had occurred while I was locked in that dungeon of a life with Keith disappeared overnight.

That night I dressed at Theo's place. I had never to his home before. He had simple taste and, apparently, loved dark woods and paintings by bohemian artists.

"My maid came in today, and so I'm sure you'll find everything in order," he said, clicking on the lamp.

"What a nice place," I told him, looking around at all the little knickknacks. He had collected many autographs from starlets and sports figures and had them all in frames in a curio cabinet.

"You really think so? Most of my friends say it's a bit stuffy in here."

"No . . . it's you."

"Well, I'm going to shower and change, and you're welcome to use my guest room. There is a bathroom in there."

"You have two bathrooms?" I asked. He laughed at me.

Of course, Molly had two bathrooms, but she had a ranch. It also had six bedrooms. However, I'd never known anyone who lived in the city to have those kinds of accommodations.

Carrying the red gown he'd picked out for me, I went into the guest room. After I showered and put on my underthings, I slid into the dress. It fit like a glove. I stood admiring it in the mirror while holding my hair up high on my head. Just then, the door opened, and Theo entered the room. My stomach jumped, but I pretended to be calm. I had wondered when the time would come that I would have to thank him for all of this, and so I figured this was it, but instead he moved up behind me and smiled into the reflection of both of us in the mirror.

"We are a handsome couple, Emma. Don't you think so?" I looked at him over my shoulder and nodded. "My mother will be very fond of you."

"I hope so."

I thought he would caress me, or maybe even kiss

my bare neck; he, instead, zipped up the dress. He took my hair, which I had piled on my head, and he let it fall around my shoulders. "Let it hang," he said.

"Okay," I agreed, barely able to contain myself. Just being in Theo's aura moved me. He was so smooth and sexy. I just wondered how much longer his being a gentleman with me would hold out.

That night, as expected, Theo's friends were stunned that he had landed a girlfriend. "And such a smart one, too," his mother said, tapping me on the shoulder and giving me a wink. I just smiled. I think I had a perpetual smile going, because by the time the evening ended, my face hurt.

"Where do you stay, Emma?" his mother asked me.

"She's from Dallas and just moved to Venice to stay with some friends during the school year, Mother. I told you that. She's a farm girl turned Bohemian," Theo said, sounding very tongue in cheek.

"Now I find it hard to believe, Theo, that you would be so brave as to step into the world of gypsies and bring one home with you," one of his friends joked.

"Oh, my Theo's very brave," I chimed in, bringing a round of unexpected laughter. For whatever reason, just that comment, just claiming Theo as *mine*, changed everything for us. At that comment, Theo kissed my hand tenderly. I'd say that was our first kiss, and it was very impressive.

"Theo tells me that you're planning to take classes here in Los Angeles," his mother said to me later that evening, while we milled around the dessert table. She had admitted earlier that she had a horrible sweet tooth, and I had worked harder than anyone there to try not to eat everything in sight. I knew my way around dinner parties, and eating like a refugee was never acceptable, yet all the fresh oysters and shrimp platters were about to drive me crazy.

"Yes," I lied.

"What are you studying here that you can't find in Texas?"

I felt a trick question coming on, and so I simply avoided it by taking a big bite from the cream puff. About that time, Theo showed up . . . right on time, as was quickly becoming his forte.

"I see you two finally gave into your true selves," he teased.

"Oh, Theo, don't tell on me," his mother said and giggled. "But you do know, after everyone leaves, I'm going to eat everything on this table," she admitted. I used the napkin to wipe my mouth while chuckling at her joke.

"Where are you staying while you're in town, child?" his mother asked. Her words came with such caring and sincerity, I almost answered her. But telling her I was staying on the street would have ruined her evening, I know.

"Well, I was thinking she would stay with me," Theo answered, slyly wrapping his arm around my waist tightly.

"She'll do no such thing. She'll stay here, if she's not going to be missed in the gypsy village." His mother was joking about the village but I could only hope she wasn't joking with the offer to stay. I was all for it but stood quietly, waiting on Theo to accept or decline it.

"It sounds wonderful. Then the two of you can become best of friends or whatever you gals do," Theo said, fanning his hand as if bored with the feminine mystique.

"Wonderful, indeed," his mother concurred, pulling

me from Theo's arms. She led me to what would become my room.

It was done. Like magic, Theo had arranged for me to stay in his parents' home while I attended classes at the local university. The next day, he brought my clothes, packed in bags, as if I had truly just arrived in town. I met his father and, in reality, was neither impressed nor not. Even when he died a year later, we all just seemed to move forward. But, anyway, during the time I was with his mother, it was an unspoken agreement that I would keep my past there . . . in the past. Theo had no worries about that; there were so many more interesting topics to talk about than my lousy life. . . .

The Vietnam War

Cassius Clay

Joanne Woodward's star on the Hollywood Walk of Fame

Elvis coming home

Ella Fitzgerald's scat sound driving me to a frenzy

And, more specifically, civil rights. That was the heated discussion of the day. Theo and I had many late-night arguments over the topic of civil rights, and in the end, I always won. My case was easy to prove . . . for obvious reasons.

"Listen here, Mr. Fairbanks," Theo's mother said one night, about three months after I moved in. She'd entered the parlor, where he and I had gone at it until nearly 2 A.M., in a *to the death* discussion about Martin Luther King being harassed for his right to speak out about what he believed. "You either marry this girl or go home . . . the neighbors are starting to talk," she said.

"Fine . . . I'll marry her," he said.

I was caught mid-sentence and left breathless.

Chapter 24

It was like a dream. All of Theo's friends, both male and female, more than accepted me, all seemingly amazed that Theo had landed a wife like me.

His constituents adored me, and he encouraged me to be outspoken about my political views, and so I was. However, on the issue of my personal life, I could tell he wanted me to draw the line, as he, too, was very private in that regard.

Our quickly planned wedding was fantasy like and took place just short of immediately. Theo hired a horse-driven carriage to pick me up at his mother's home and rode with me to the church, where we exchanged our vows.

Lifting my white veil, he kissed me on both cheeks after we were pronounced Assemblyman Theo Fairbanks and wife. He had been an assemblyman for the past three years.

That night we cruised to Catalina Island.

"Theo, I'm very happy," I told him after he toasted *us*.

"I'm glad, Emma, because you've been so wonderful for me . . . and to me," he told me.

"Do you love me?" I asked him. He smiled coquettishly and kissed my cheek tenderly before taking my glass and setting it on the small table. He took my hand and led me to our marriage bed, pulling back the heavy comforter. He sat down and urged me to sit on his lap.

"Do you want to know how much I love you?"

"Yes," I purred, thinking about how it would be to feel him inside me. Theo was such a handsome man, mature and, no doubt, experienced. He was quite a bit older than I was—I was twenty-four—but it never seemed to be an issue between us. I figured that was the reason he never spent time groping me or begging for sexual favors. He slid my shear robe from my shoulders, and it fell softly around his feet.

"I had your personal files sealed. No one will ever know who your mother was. No one but me . . ." he said, staring through me now.

I felt the shiver in my bones.

He knew.

My mouth dropped open . . . so far that he actually closed it with his soft hands.

Sliding me from his lap, he laid me on the bed, removed my slippers, and covered me up, kissing my forehead tenderly. I could tell he wasn't about to lie down next to me, and I felt my eyes burn. I was confused and upset. Was he rejecting me because I was black? Was he no better than Keith . . . just richer? What had he married me for?

"Why?" I began, but my words choked on my tears.

"Emerald . . . sweet Emerald, as wise as you are, you are so very naive about matters of life," he began, and then, hovering over me, he whispered in my ear. "It's not your race that repulses me. It's your sex."

He smiled at me. His eyes were sad just a little, for he knew he had hurt me deeper than he had planned. All this time what I had mistaken for respect was nothing more than another smoke screen. My husband was homosexual.

I cried myself to sleep that night, hot silent tears that I knew he could not hear, even from his adjoining room.

Chapter 25

Married life and life with Theo were two very different yet interesting things. To the public, we were more than the perfect couple: attentive, sophisticated, and devoted to one another. But in private, we were simply Theo and Emma, two people with two different lives, sharing a common goal . . . and that goal was clearly undefined. I'd have to say, looking back, that the goal probably was Theo's career; we just didn't know that yet . . . or hadn't accepted it as the cold, hard facts.

I had taken a few classes during our engagement but quickly dropped them after we married. There wasn't much Theo wanted me to do in the public eye that he wasn't closely associated with, so I stayed pretty close to the political scene. Even his friends and colleagues at the university found it interesting that he would rather have me at a political conference than in school. I personally think it was because Theo's friends and I had all become rather chummy, and I know that made him nervous.

"You talk too much," he told me one night, while brushing his teeth, getting ready for bed. We had houseguests and so were sharing a room that night. That was what we normally did to keep up appearances.

"I didn't say anything. They were the ones to jump to the conclusions," I defended. My dinner conversation had grown a bit controversial and heated, and now Theo and I were arguing. I really didn't even remember how the argument started, but we were going at it.

I jumped up, undressed quickly, and turned on the bathwater. It was then that I noticed Theo had stopped speaking and was staring at me as I bent over, naked, warming my hand under the water flow. "What?" I asked him, noticing his head cock to the side slightly and then straighten back up.

"Why do you do that?" he asked me, pointing his toothbrush at me.

"What? Take a bath? Run the water? Get naked? Which?" I asked, standing now and facing him, with my hands on my hips.

"All of the above," he answered, rolling his eyes and quickly leaving the bathroom, with a full blush on his cheeks. I couldn't help but laugh. I had turned Theo on, and he was angry about it. It hit my funny bone, and I teased him the rest of the night.

We never talked about his preferences much, but I couldn't resist challenging them at every opportunity after that night.

Sometimes I would slip into bed with him, naked. Sometimes I would all but molest him while he slept, but to no avail; none of it got me anywhere. Theo was determined not to have sex with me.

"When are the two of you going to give me grandchildren?" his mother asked one afternoon, while we golfed. I had taken up the sport and rather enjoyed it.

Or maybe it was just spending time with Mrs. Fairbanks that I enjoyed so much.

I chuckled at her question and ignored it, not answering her overtly.

"That's what I thought," she said, with a smirk.

"We will one day, Mother Fairbanks," I told her, noticing her disappointed expression.

"Emma." She called my name in such a tone, I had to give her my attention. "I know it's hard being his wife," she said.

"No, it's not. I really love Theo. He's—"

"He's not giving you what a husband should. I know that. It was hard at first to accept the truth . . . but I know it's the truth."

I didn't say anything and fought with all my might not to show any expression on my face.

"You don't have to say anything. I know the truth about my son. Well, I didn't know for a very long time, and I thought I was wrong when the two of you got married. I was thinking, leave the boy alone; he's a slow starter," she went on, revealing to me the thoughts she had regarding her son. "I mean, you are a very"—she fumbled for words "—alive kind of woman, and, well, if he were sleeping with you, you two would have children by now . . . or at least would be working on some, if you get my meaning." She winked.

"Mrs. Fairbanks, I . . ."

She moved past me, as if done talking and thinking about the subject. I knew she had mixed feelings. I started walking behind her to the next hole. We got there, and she took her swing and then looked at me.

"Are you planning to take a lover? What am I asking? Women never plan that kind of thing."

"I would never plan that kind of thing," I said, admitting to what she had alluded to about her son's and my marital bed, yet not, at the same time. She shook her head and then patted my shoulder.

"He's very fond of you."

"And I'm fond of him, too," I admitted. She smiled, happy to hear it.

I loved Theo's mother, and when she died unexpectedly, I grieved very much.

Chapter 26

On November 22, 1963, we all were gathered in Dallas, Texas. Theo's campaign for Congress was in full swing, and following the president around made for easy access to voters. We'd made many trips. I had to admit that I enjoyed the travel. Personally, I enjoyed our trips to New York the most. Theo was generous, and my shopping habits often left us needing to ship my packages home separately from our luggage. Theo kept me more than happy materially. I think he, somewhere deep inside, feared betrayal—that I might reveal his dirty secret. But then again, he had me by the screws both coming and going, so there was no chance of that. What I think Theo never understood was that he had become my friend. Despite all else, I respected his political views and enjoyed his friendship. We had an arrangement, like many marriages.

Now I found myself in Dallas, lodging at the Dallas Hotel. I had told Theo about Molly, and he urged me to resist the temptation to visit the ranch. He never forbade me to do anything, but when he *urged* me, I knew he meant for me to take heed. The boredom of sitting in the hotel room, however, made his wishes hard to obey.

"Why not just go spend some more money?" his personal attendant, Jared, suggested. I didn't care for him much, although Theo had assured me my dislike for him was invented to sooth my feelings of rejection. I thought Jared was Theo's secret male lover, so I didn't care for him. I also sometimes felt alone and unattractive because Theo never made any sexual moves on me.

"There is nothing going on between me and Jared. I'm much more discreet than that," he told me one night. Even after all this time, Theo and I still had to sleep together for appearances' sake when company came from out of town, and on those nights, we usually argued, and I would never let an occasion go by without making a sexual advance on my husband. Generally, I slept in my wing of the house, and Theo slept on his end.

"Theo, don't lie to me. I can see it in his nasty little eyes, and besides, he treats me like a piece of shit. I bet you told him about me, didn't you?"

"No, and how many times do I have to tell you not to be so crass?" he counseled, turning his back to me. I reached around him, stroking his manhood. He hated when I did that, too.

"What are you trying to accomplish?" he asked me.

"I don't know . . . but damned if I wasn't gonna give it a shot," I snapped.

This day in Dallas I was bored out of my mind and begged Theo to allow me to at least drive by Molly's ranch to see if she still lived there, but he refused to allow it.

"You're just discontent. Perhaps Jared is right, and you should maybe go shopping or something," Theo told me. Jared chuckled. I nearly flew into a rage.

"What are you laughing at, asshole queer?" I snapped.

"Oh, my gosh, how juvenile you are," Jared retorted, smacking his full lips. "Did you hear what she called me?"

"Listen, you two cut it out. Do something better with your time," Theo barked and then headed into the bedroom. Something was bothering him, I could tell. Actually, something seemed to be bothering us all. The air had a sense of change brewing. I followed my husband into the bedroom. He was lying on the bed, with his back to me.

"Theo, are you okay?" I asked. "I'm sorry, I called Jared that. I'm sorry, I . . ."

He turned to me. "No, I'm not . . ." he answered.

"What's wrong?"

"I don't know. Maybe I'm missing my mother . . . I don't know. It's silly really," he said, attempting a light chuckle. I hugged him, and for the first time in weeks, he hugged me back. It wasn't as if he didn't like me. It was just that I had been on the make again, and so he'd taken to avoiding all physical contact with me. But today he hugged me back, and so I kissed him, surprised that he returned my affection. We kissed a long time before he looked at me.

"You are such a good friend to me, Emma. Sometimes I want to spank you, but for the most part . . . I love you very much," he said.

"You love me?" I asked. It wasn't as if he'd said those words before . . . not like that, anyway.

"Of course, I do. You're my . . . my girlfriend," he said, blushing slightly.

"Oh, Theo, now see. That makes me so happy," I told him, hugging him again. This time his hands wandered down my back. I didn't look at him but kept my face buried in his shoulder while he unzipped my dress and unhooked my bra.

"Are you sure you want to do this?" I asked him then.

"I'm not a virgin, Emma. I've been with a woman before . . . it's just not my preference," he said.

After undressing, we fell into the bed together, groping and kissing each other like high schoolers. I remembered how unnatural the kiss between Sade and me had felt, but it wasn't the same with Theo. His kiss was good, soft, and . . . sweet. He knew how to kiss me in a way that made me want more. I didn't for a moment think outside this moment, as I truly had no concept of his other life. It wasn't as if there were books available for me to read and learn all the ins and outs of homosexuality, and Theo was discreet to the utmost. Essentially, he could have just as easily been impotent for the last three years, as there was no flamboyant acting or outlandish habits, like wearing my clothes or make-up. Theo was very manly in all ways, and for this moment, he was my man. At this point, we had been married three years and had never consummated the marriage.

I shivered under his touch, the touch I had craved for so long. He could tell how much I wanted him, as I quickly arched upward to meet his readiness. When he entered me, our eyes met, and I knew our relationship had instantly changed. I knew in my heart that if Theo never touched me again, he would know my love and remember it always. Deeply, he explored my body, grinding his teeth and moaning softly in my ear, saying my name over and over. Although I didn't feel anything that resembled the Fourth of July between my legs, I felt as though Theo's love was sincere. He'd given me something that cost him more to give than to get, and no one had ever done that much for me. When he released inside me, I held his face and kissed his lips. "I will always love you, Theo," I promised.

Suddenly, the door burst open. It was Jared. Frozen, he stared at us coupled in intercourse, and then, as if suddenly remembering why he had entered our private space, he exploded with the news. "The president has been shot!"

Chapter 27

Theo's appointment to the House of Representatives came the following year, and we quickly moved into the lifestyle that came with the title and the quest for the Senate. That was what was next for Theo, and I promised to stand beside him, no matter what.

We hired staff to care for our large home, and I felt guilty a little bit for living so high and mighty, as my mother would call it. But then again, I knew she was looking down on me, proud that I had finally managed to get this right. I had done what Mr. Garcia had said and had gotten through the tough times.

But still, something was missing in my life, and although I hadn't spelled it out to Theo, I knew he knew what it was.

As I had imagined, our life together had changed a little since that historical day in Dallas, Texas. We had not been sexually intimate again; however, we now shared a room and slept together more often. Theo seemed to adore me, and I truly felt the same way about him. Giggling, we would share gossip like playmates. He finally confided in me who his lover was, and I was shocked that such a high-ranking figure was homosexual. It was hard to keep a straight face when seeing him in public with his wife.

Jared, who obviously had had a secret crush on my husband, had quit not too long after that day in Dallas and was replaced by a woman, who stayed in the position during Theo's entire tenure in politics. I liked her. She did her job and didn't let things get too personal between herself and Theo. I'm not sure if she knew he was gay, but if she did, she never said anything or acted any certain way when in his presence—or mine.

Theo traveled a lot now, and I didn't go along as often as I did when he was an assemblyman. The world was changing, and the issues being dealt with in the House were much more complicated than they used to be. There was no room for an opinionated loudmouth like me.

This time while Theo was in the east, he did something for me that I would never forget.

"Ma'am, there's a call for you. I believe it's Congressman Fairbanks," the butler informed me.

"Thank you, Maxwell." I picked up the phone. "Hello, darling," I teased. I could almost see Theo's blush through the phone.

"Stop that, Emma. I called for something important."

I sat up straight, bracing myself. "What is it?"

"A car will be delivering your present tonight . . . so be ready."

"A present," I said, sighing with relief at the same time.

"Yes, and if you were thinking of trying to start a fight about something ridiculous when I get home, this will certainly change your mind."

"Will it cause us to make love?" I asked, knowing the answer.

"Emma . . . stop. Just be ready," he said. I giggled and hung up.

A present . . .

About eight that evening, as promised, a car pulled up outside. I went to the door to await my gift. Out stepped Josie from the back of the limo. I screamed and ran to the car, hugging her as tight as I could. Our tears fell like water, and I realized Theo was, indeed, the best friend I could ever have.

Theo had no worries about me trying to molest him when he returned. I was too busy spending days and nights with Josie. Maybe it had been a plot on his part to distract me from bothering him, but for whatever reason he did it, I was thankful.

Aunt Rebecca was doing well, as hateful as always, but glad that Josie was coming out west to be with me. Despite how long I had been married to such a public figure, I was surprised that Josie still hadn't realized that fact until she was visited by an official-looking delivery man who presented her with a one-way ticket to California.

It wasn't as if there were many pictures of me in the paper. Theo wanted to avoid my being recognized that way, and with my past sealed and filed away, so far there hadn't been anyone from the grave of Emerald Jackson coming back to haunt Emma Fairbanks. I had made it; I had successfully crossed over and passed with the help of Theo. I didn't think often anymore about how it felt to be white; it came natural for me. These days it was more of a challenge to just keep myself out of a jam.

Surprisingly enough, Josie wasn't angry about it, either. She seemed more than happy to be called my maid, when in fact she did very little housekeeping, short of cleaning her own quarters. She joined a church in Inglewood and every Sunday was driven in and then picked up. In terms of public appearances, Theo realized it was advantageous for me to attend services with her from time to time. It showed my community spirit in the heat of the civil rights movement, which still raged on, and, of course, it kept me happy, which kept me out of his hair.

On some nights, Josie and I would listen to the radio and dance to the latest music. She would teach me steps she had learned from her friends in town. It was nice being able to have a life vicariously through her.

She admitted to me that for years, she had been jealous of me, but after hearing about some of my misadventures, she quickly rethought things.

"Damn," she gasped after hearing about my time with Keith. "You should have shot his ass."

"I wanted to, but then, in a way, if I hadn't been with Keith, I wouldn't have met Theo."

"But, Em'rald, you killed your baby."

"I know, and I know Mama was angry with me for getting rid of her grandbaby. But eventually, I think she forgave me."

"But then again, maybe that's why you ain't had another try."

That's when I realized that Josie had no idea about my and Theo's sexless marriage.

"Or maybe Theo is just waiting for the right time," I covered.

"True, true . . ." she said right as Theo entered the room where we were. I had made a large fire, and we were enjoying freshly popped corn. "When are ya'll gonna have some kids, Theo?" she asked just as Theo threw a handful of popcorn in his mouth. He began to choke and turn red. I jumped up to pat his back.

"I guess no time soon then, huh?" Josie said, sipping her tea and turning back to the fire.

We wound up fixing up servants' quarters for Josie. In spite of our disagreements as children, and even though she was far from a servant, Josie became a good friend to me.

Chapter 28

The novelty of having Josie there had worn off, and I was back involved in politics. She had been a ploy, and later I saw through Theo's plot to keep me busy while he went on with his career. But I was hip to his jive now; again, I was back on track, trying to get in on everything Theo was doing . . . much to his dismay.

So much was going on in the world. Even the music showed signs of change. One could feel it in the vast difference in genres. From folk to Motown, everyone had a story to tell.

There were so many sides to be on, it was difficult to think straight. I had started attending roundtable discussions at the local branch of the NAACP, of which Josie was a member. I joined many groups, including the affirmative action committee, the school board, and other types of committees that would allow me direct contact with minorities. Theo and I fought constantly over the issues, and for the first time, he asked me to scale down my involvement. Tensions were high, and I feared a civil war in my own home.

"I can't," I told him.

"You have to. You're too outspoken, and it's hurting me," he told me.

I paced the bedroom, listening to him speak about the Conservative Party breathing down his neck. "Who gives a damn what I say, Theo? Since when have you cared?" I finally blurted out.

"I've always cared. There's just never been a time like this where there was so much going on. The last *discourse* . . ." He used the word *discourse* loosely, as if just the thought of my attempting to be a public speaker made his flesh crawl. There were still a few speaking skills I'd yet to master. "It had my people ringing my phone off the hook!"

"I can't just sit quietly by and say nothing when there is so much injustice in the world. Malcolm X has been assassinated. Don't you care?"

It was hard to pretend that nothing bothered me. It was difficult to sit back and watch things just happen. I felt so very out of control.

"Emma . . . it's not that I don't care, but listen to me. We can't get involved with every situation. I don't want you getting involved with every civil rights issue that comes up."

Theo sat and watched as I paced up and down the bedroom floor. "What if it drops in my lap?"

"If your lap is home, how could that happen?"

"I'm sorry, Theo, but I have needs."

"And I'm sorry about that. I'm sorry that you are left with needs that you cannot satisfy, but . . ."

"What kind of comment was that? That was a sexual comment, and I was not talking about that."

"Neither was I!" he yelled. I was stunned into silence. Theo never raised his voice to me. I quickly went to his side, sitting next to him on the bed. "It's always one thing or the other with you. My God, you are so very limited!"

Limited! It was funny how what once made me alluring—my passion for sex and politics—now only made me seem retarded and stifled in my ability to think outside those two topics.

"Theo, I'm sorry. I'm . . . I'm frustrated," I confessed.

"You're always frustrated . . . what's new!" he growled, jumping to his feet and storming toward the door. He stopped before leaving.

Theo was tiring of me, I could tell. He had done everything to keep me happy, and he was out of options. The only one he had left he knew he could not do . . . and that was to give me a family of my own to care about and fuss over. We both knew it was true . . . It was time for me to become a mother. I knew it. He knew it. But did he love me enough? That was the question.

"I have to go to Washington for several weeks, Emma, and . . ."—he paused—"we'll discuss some things when I get back."

"Some things?" I asked.

"Some things that I think you need. I . . ." He paused.

"All right, Theo . . ." I interrupted, sensing the difficulty he was having. It broke my heart to think that Theo didn't want to have a child with me. Again, after all these years of forgetting about my blackness, because it was locked away in a file . . . it had come back to haunt us.

Josie sensed the tension in the house and attempted to distract me by sharing more of her personal life with me. I was unaware she had gotten serious with a young man from her church.

"So are you two going to get married?" I asked her as we shopped on Rodeo Drive.

"Maybe."

"Well, I want to meet him," I insisted.

"I am not taking you anywhere near him."

"Why?"

"You done lost your mind if you think I want him knowing you are related to me."

"Don't tell him," I said, licking my ice cream cone. "Tell you what. I'll just put on some casual clothes and like maybe a wig or something, and we'll go down to—"

"Watts," she said, answering my unasked question as to where the young man lived.

"Watts and check him out. I mean, he needs to pass my test."

Josie laughed. "Like you know a good man when you meet one."

"I do . . . I have Theo, don't I?" I said.

"Riiiight." She chuckled, making me wonder for a moment if she knew the truth about Theo's orientation.

I took another lick off my cone and tossed it in the trash before entering a wig shop.

"You are serious, aren't you?" Josie asked me.

"As a heart attack!"

"I'm sure Congressman Fairbanks gave you some instructions. . . ."

"His name is Theo, and he ain't my daddy!"

"Old enough ta be . . ." Josie giggled.

By the time we got to Watts, I was looking like a black girl. I had heard that Lena Horne had used a bronzing powder to darken her skin to be black enough for Hollywood, and so I quickly acquired some of the same stuff. With my hair tucked under a short, curly wig, I donned a pair of sunglasses, and away we went.

Reaching his neighborhood, Josie parked the car, which Theo had purchased for her. We usually took her car when going out together. Stepping out, we together walked the block to her boyfriend's apartment building. Josie was full of giggles when we knocked on the door. When the young man answered, he grinned from ear to ear at the sight of Josie, and I felt warm inside knowing she had someone who really cared. I could tell.

We stayed at his house until nearly dark, having dinner and visiting, but around eight or so, a commotion in the streets drew our attention.

The Watts Riots began that day and lasted for six days longer. And during that time, my life again took a dramatic turn. Rushing to the streets, everyone began going crazy. I wasn't sure when it started, but by the time Josie and I realized what we were in the middle of, it was scary. Taking a bat in hand, Josie's boyfriend attempted to escort us back to our car but failed, being dragged into a fight. I could feel Josie's helplessness while watching her young man take punches like a professional boxer.

"We have to get out of here," I told her.

"I'm scared, Em'rald," she whined.

"Just hold on to me." And she did. We held each other tight while trying to get back to her car but only ended up farther and farther from it, being pushed and shoved in the darkness. My bad sense of direction played a part in getting us turned totally around.

It was like a war zone.

Suddenly, I noticed a young black soldier being attacked by three white men. He was clearly outnumbered. Perhaps I was caught up in my civic duty and perhaps just the fervor of the moment, but something inside me just made me want to help him. I pulled away from Josie. I ran toward the fight. She screamed for me to come back, but I was too far gone to stop. As I approached, my wig and glasses fell off. "Stop beating him!" I screamed. "Stop!"

The one that didn't recognize me drew his hand back to strike me, but the young soldier decked him. The other men ran off. I grabbed the soldier's arm to pull him to safety, and that's when I saw his face clearly. Although he was thirteen years older, he still looked the same.

"Noah!" I screamed.

"Em'rald?"

Lifting me off my feet, Noah carried me back to where Josie stood, scared out of her mind. Maybe seeing Noah scared her even more, because I swore she was going to faint. And before I realized it, Noah had us both caught up in his embrace, lifted off our feet, carried like rag dolls.

Somehow, we found the car. The windows were busted out, but we got in, Noah took the keys from Josie's shaking hands, and we drove off.

Chapter 29

I wasn't sure where we were, but I knew we were still in the middle of the action. Noah parked the car and helped us out of the glass-ridden interior and up the few steps to a porch.

"My friends live here," he said, sounding vague and offering no more information about his personal life. I caught his eyes covering me, and I returned the eye coverage. Unbelievable but true, it was Noah . . . my dearest friend, my husband. Suddenly, as my life flashed before my eyes in a delayed replay fashion, I grew angry, seeing the glistening of a small chain around his neck. It hung there, in addition to his dog tag. I knew immediately what it was and snatched it from his neck, breaking the clasp.

The suddenness of my violence shocked him, and he gasped, reaching for where the locket once hung. "You're late! You're very late!" I yelled, tossing the locket to the ground. My eyes burned with hot tears, and my lips buckled in anger. Yes, Noah was too damn late to do what he had promised. I had lived white much longer than I ever had dreamed I would, and now, I wasn't sure I could go back to black even if I wanted to.

Josie was grabbing my arm to keep me from flipping out further when the door opened. A nice, calm-looking older woman had opened the door.

"Ferrell here?" Noah asked politely, despite the fact that just seconds ago his eyes had blazed with angry surprise at my reaction to our reunion. The woman looked at his torn shirt and at the two of us, Josie and me. We looked rumpled and disheveled.

"Oh Lord, ya'll done been in the fightin'. I saw it on the television. Come on in and rest yourselves," she said, opening the screen wide and allowing us to come in.

As I got closer, I saw her get a better look at me, and so I ducked my eyes as I went in. My hair was pulled into a tight bun on the top of my head for the sake of the wig, but I was certain she was looking at its texture and the color of my eyes, despite the dark coloring I had on my skin.

Inside, I sat on the large black sofa. Her home was furnished very modern, and it was comfortable. I immediately noticed her bookshelf filled with books, which I knew would hold my interest. I wondered if she perhaps was a teacher.

Noah had yet to sit. He stood fiddling with the chain that had held the locket. The woman noticed. "Did your necklace get broken . . . how awful and such a beautiful locket, too," she said, taking it from him and disappearing with it into one of the back rooms. "Just have a seat and wait for Ferrell. You realize, you all might end up staying over. I'm sure they are going to quarantine the area off . . . won't be no leaving tonight!" she called out.

"I can't stay over," I whispered loudly. "I'm sure my . . . I'm sure I'll be missed."

"Shoulda thought of that before you disobeyed," Josie whispered back. The woman returned, holding out the locket which she had repaired. Noah, who still stood staring at me, pointed at me so that she could hand it to me. My heart tightened.

"It belongs to her," he said. The woman quickly turned to me and smiled, trying not to ask the questions that immediately filled her mind.

"Here, honey," she said. Her voice showed her discomfort, and after handing it to me, I was sure she could see where the make-up ended at my wrist and my lighter skin tones showed. She pulled back quickly, sighing then a ragged breath. "I'm going to go in the kitchen and cook up a little something."

"I'll help you, Mrs. . . ." Josie jumped up, knowing Noah and I needed a moment or two or a billion.

"My name is Loni Price. Just call me Loni," she told Josie as they headed toward what looked like a large kitchen, which perhaps had a breakfast nook attached. Loni was the mother of Ferrell, Noah's best friend. I hadn't figured that Negros were living as nice as this woman was. I wondered if perhaps I had been stereotyping blacks, if my assumptions about their downtrodden existence had made them more pitiable than they should have been. Not everyone was destitute just because they were black. I had never stopped to reason that simply because they weren't the Sammy Davis Jrs. or Nat King Coles of the world didn't mean they weren't able to be educated or make a decent living. I had gotten so caught up in my mission—to prove I was black—I had lost focus on reality. Being black wasn't always a battle. I could see that now.

Of course, the rioting outside wasn't helping, but I could see that much in just this short time in Mrs. Price's house.

"Noah," I called. He looked at me. He'd been

looking off, maybe thinking similar thoughts, maybe wondering why my skin had been painted, maybe wondering what Mrs. Price was cooking. . . .

I had to realize that not everyone thought about me all the time.

I held out the locket for him to take it back. He rolled his eyes, and then, pushing off the wall in a reluctant body language, he snatched it from my hand. "This here has been my good luck charm . . . up till day today, anyway. You probably done jinxed it."

"Noah, what are you doing here?"

"I'm in the service. I was down at the recruitment center . . . which is why I'm in uniform." He looked down at his torn shirt. "Tow up my damn shirt. Crazy ass white folks . . . always trying to beat up on a Nigga anytime they think they can get away with it," he cussed under his breath.

"So, this was a coincidence?" I asked him.

"I knew you lived here, if that's what you're asking."

"You knew?"

He smiled and said nothing more for Mrs. Price had returned with cups of coffee. "I wasn't sure if you drank coffee, young lady, but I know our soldier here does. He comes by every morning to have coffee and talk." She smiled at me sweetly. I caught her eyes, and she winked ever so covertly. I know my mouth moved to form the word *mama* instead of *thank you,* but she didn't seem to notice. "You're welcome," she said. I pulled my dirty jacket closer around me. She must have noticed and offered me the bathroom.

"When you and your cousin get ready, just let me know, and you two can shower and put on something of mine. I might be a bit big for you . . ." she said, noting my petite frame.

"It's all right. That would be wonderful," I quickly answered. Her phone rang.

She answered it. "Hello . . . Ferrell, yes. What's happening? Noah is here . . . quarantine." She nodded in our direction. "Well, that's what I told them . . . burning . . . fires everywhere, ump, ump, ump . . . ," she added.

I looked at Noah, who was listening, before he quickly turned on Mrs. Price's television.

Josie came from the kitchen, waving for me to follow her. I did. "This house is really big. She's got a basement and everything . . . a backyard. It's the biggest house I've ever been in . . . well, besides yours," she added, giggling under her breath.

"Josie, I can't be here . . . not with Noah . . . not like this," I said, pointing down at my getup.

"After you shower, you can just tell Mrs. Price who you are. She's already asked me a ton of questions about you. She saw your green eyes and wondered how we were related . . . she already knows something don't smell right."

"I can't do this . . . This isn't how I planned."

"Since when has your life gone like you've planned? I have to call my boyfriend, see if he got his head cracked. That's all I need is to have his head cracked," Josie then said, wandering toward the living room to use the phone after Mrs. Price hung up. I followed her back.

"So, Noah, you can probably leave without being stopped, and maybe even make it back to your hotel, beings as how you're in the military," Mrs. Price was saying. "But these gals here . . . well, it won't be so easy for you to travel with them. It's urged that all civilians stay inside until the National Guard"—Mrs. Price turned to me—"or your parents . . ."

"My parents are no longer living," I answered.

"Where do you live?" she asked.

"Bel . . . Inglewood," I lied. I figured there was no

sense telling her the truth about me living in one of the most expensive communities in Southern California. After I washed all this bronzing from me, she would have enough questions, and I would answer them all at one time. "I'm about ready for that shower now," I told her.

The water poured over my head, washing away the soot, the dirt, the mask. I felt clean in the flesh, but my spirit ached me. I knew when I walked out, my life would again hit me in the face. All the prayers, all my desires, all my confusions and convictions would come into play all at once.

Stepping out of the bathroom, wrapped in the towel provided by Mrs. Price, I met the older woman in the room, laying out a colorful dashiki, much like the one I saw Josie wearing after her shower. I had never worn one before.

"I'm sure you'll fit . . ." She stopped short, looking at what I knew appeared to be a white girl coming from her bathroom.

"I'm sure I can, too," I answered, removing the towel from my head and allowing my overgrown hair to fall around my shoulders. She looked me up and down.

"I thought I knew you," she said. I was unable to read her expression, and I worried.

"You do?" I asked her.

"You're the congressman's wife?"

"I . . . yes, I am." I quickly pulled the large garment over me, allowing the towel to drop from underneath.

"You're his token to the black community . . . white as you may be," she added, jerking her neck. "How are you supposed to know the needs of black people?" she started.

"Well, I—"

"We feel insulted by you. Did you know that? This is his best effort in trying to get close to us black people . . . getting some loudmouthed white Texan woman who probably only knows about collards because her maid used to cook them . . . shit," she snapped, fanning her hand.

"Insulted!" I defended. "Mrs. Price, I don't speak out for civil rights from ignorance. I fully know the needs of the black people. . . ."

"Honey . . . you don't know shit. The fact that you felt you needed to lie about having black relatives and painted your skin out of fear of even coming into our neighborhood tells me you don't know . . ."

"I didn't want to be recognized," I confessed.

"Recognized as what? A white woman . . . honey . . . Look in the mirror. That is what you are!"

"Please, Mrs. Price . . . hear me out. Congressman Fairbanks is a liberal. I know he puts on a conservative front, but he has his reasons. He is trying to reach the Senate and may one day run for the presidency. With me by his side, he'll make changes. I can assure you of that."

"So you plannin' to be the next Eleanor Roosevelt? Running the White House from home?" she asked slyly. "Trust me, honey . . . his being president is not gonna do nothing for us . . . it's not going to change anything. I'm sure he's very impressed by your willingness to step over to the colored side of town every now and then and do your little spiel about the need for equality. And . . . sure, you can talk the talk, but until you step into my black skin, you can't walk the walk," she went on. "Now . . . if he were to have married a black women, then I might have been impressed with Mr. Fairbanks's efforts to reach his black constituents.

But then, too, if he had married a black women, chances are . . . he wouldn't be Congressman Fairbanks."

Just then, Noah came into the room. His eyes caught me out of the corner, and he quickly diverted his gaze.

"Mrs. Price, you have to believe me. Congressman Fairbanks is as liberal as . . ." I thought about Theo's lover, another politician hiding behind a conservative platform. "As they come," I finished.

She harrumphed and gave Noah a once-over. "And you gonna get your ass in more trouble than you might wanna be in, running with this white woman here," she told him.

"She won't be white too much longer," he said, with conviction. I had to wonder if he and Josie had been talking while I took my shower.

"Well, until then, I want you all in the basement," said Mrs. Price. "I'm not having my reputation tarnished by the likes of this woman in my house. If my club members found out I had Congressman Fairbanks's wife here . . . ohhh Lawd, I'd have a riot right here in my living room."

She left the room. Silence covered Noah and me, as if hearing the fact that I was married said out loud again hit us. "So . . . uhh . . . the basement. Have you been down there?" I asked. He nodded slowly.

"I'm gonna wash up, and then I'm going to come down there," he said. I nodded. "Em'rald, we gone get through this okay. Even if I have to take you back to your house myself. I ain't scared of no roadblocks."

"I know, but I'll wait a while longer. I'm just not ready to get out in all that mess right now. Theo isn't even home, and I'm probably not even missed . . . It's not like anyone there really cares about me."

"Your husband cares."

I laughed. "Yeah, he cares." As I passed Noah, my

hand ran across his chest. I don't know why I did it, but I instantly regretted it as Noah grabbed my hand and squeezed it tightly. The tears left my eyes before I could stop them. I cried for Noah, for me, for Theo, for Mrs. Price, for love.

The basement was comfortable. There were blankets that covered the walls and large pillows on the floor. It resembled an oriental opium den, the kind I had only seen in pictures. Josie had stayed upstairs with Mrs. Price; they seemed to hit it off right away. Me, I decided to stay out of her way. I could tell she didn't really dislike me as much as what I stood for in her mind, and I wasn't sure that if I had told her I was really black, that would have helped.

Soon Noah came down, with two plates of food. He sat down on the floor next to me. He wore a white T-shirt and cuffed Levi's, no doubt belonging to his friend Ferrell. Noah's hair was cut close to his head, and he was clean shaven. I wanted to touch his face, the smooth skin, but I knew it would be like a drug, and once I touched, I would not be able to keep my hands off.

When he uncovered the plates, the wonderful smells filled my senses. "Mrs. Price hoped that you could eat this soul food . . . She knew you might be used to more fancy things," he said, sounding tongue in cheek. I rolled my eyes. "Josie already told me she does the cooking at your place."

"My place . . ." I repeated, chuckling at how simply he described my home. It was a palace compared to where he and I had started out.

Picking up the neck bone by hand, taking a bite, I savored the flavor of the meat. It wasn't what I would have expected Mrs. Price to prepare as a light summertime meal, but then again, I had a feeling she was trying to impress me with as ethnic a dish as she could think of. We both must have been starving, because we ate in silence. With my belly full, I fell back on my elbows and sighed a contented sigh. Noah sat his plate to the side and then did the same to mine.

"I can't believe this day. It's unbelievable, all of it," I admitted. He smiled and shook his head, too. I could tell Noah had much to say but refused to reveal anything. "Don't you think it's like a miracle?"

"Not really, but it's a coincidence, to be sure," he said, licking his fingers and then wiping them on the Levi's.

"Noah, why didn't you come find me?" I asked finally. He didn't look at me at first, and then, glancing over his shoulder, he just smiled.

"Em'rald, do you have any idea how much life and times have changed since we were kids? I looked for you often. And I thought about you all the time," he said, holding up the locket, which he had put back around his neck. "But things change. . . . People change."

"But a promise is a promise and . . ."

"And a vow is a vow . . . if you want to talk about promises."

I knew he was referring to our marriage, and so, again, we fell into silence and deep, soul-searching thought. I knew both of us felt the same way about how our reunion was supposed to be. It was supposed to be fantastic, otherworldly . . . perfect. But instead, it was filled with bittersweet words, with double meanings, hurt feelings, and a smoldering passion, which both of us seemed too afraid to even address. No man had ever made me feel the way Noah had, and being married to Theo, I could think of nothing other than that fact right now. It didn't matter that I had been a young girl at the time and now I was a full-grown woman. I had known what bliss was even then, and if only I could have a smidgen of it again, I would be ever so thankful.

How could I make Noah believe how he'd been on my mind recently? How much I dreamed of him alone in my bed at night? How could I prove to Noah that despite my marriage to Theo, he was the man I really loved?

Noah was right however. Times had changed, and now our love was even more *forbidden* than it had been that day in his room. Back then, we had been too young for it, and now he was too black and I was too white for it . . . leaving out the fact, of course, that I was in a sexless marriage to a homosexual Congressional representative.

I sat up and reached for the locket. It looked good around his neck . . . perfect. I fondled it. He took my hand.

"We can't go that far anymore, Em'rald. We're not married . . . we never really were. So we can't . . ." He closed his eyes. "We can't go that far anymore. I got a girl now and . . ."

"I'm your girl," I whispered. My words were weak from holding back tears. He shook his head.

"And you got a husband and . . ."

"I understand that," I lied, pulling my hand back. He reached for it and kissed my palm and then my wrist. I pulled my arm back and tucked it into my lap. He cleared his throat. Looking around, he spotted Ferrell's radio and turned it on. Ferrell already had it set on a rock and roll station that played many of the R & B songs that were out now.

"Have you been okay?" he asked me.

"No . . . well, yes . . . yes and no," I answered.

"Em'rald," he began and then shook his head, laughing.

"What? Can I help it if I've had a hard time? Life

hasn't been simple. When my mother gave me away, she picked the craziest white people in the world . . . ," I told him.

"Really? I always thought the Griffiths were all right kinda people . . . for white folks."

I shook my head fervidly. "No, they weren't. The only thing normal about them was their dog."

"Well, tell me all about it," he said, settling on his elbow.

I laid down on the big pillow. "I don't think we have time. . . ."

"Hell, ain't no fool going out tonight. We got all the time in the world." He grinned, and my love for him was refreshed. "Come on now. You can talk to me."

"Well, let me start from the beginning. First, the Griffiths never took me to St. Louis, like they told my mama . . . ," I began. "Do you love her?" I asked.

"Who?" he asked, looking confused.

"Your girl."

"Do you love your husband?" he asked me.

I couldn't answer. The word meant something different for Theo and me than it did for Noah and his girl. I knew that much, and there was no way I was going to explain how different. What Theo and I had wasn't common, and so I knew it wouldn't be fair to Theo to measure him on the common scale.

Noah kissed me, and the world stopped turning suddenly. All my thoughts disappeared faster than any drug could make happen. My thoughts of Theo were filed accordingly and sealed . . . just like my past, safe and sound, where no one could investigate them any further.

I wrapped my arms around Noah's neck and kept the kiss going for as long as I could before he pulled back. I'm sure he could see the hunger in my eyes, the want, the loneliness.

All I could hope for, however, was that behind all that, he saw my true feelings . . . the never-ending love I had for him, pure and unadulterated, although, yes, I was another man's wife.

"Tell me about your life since we saw each other last, Em'rald," he said then. I didn't realize then that Noah had never answered me about his girl. I figured he must have loved her, but our relationship was like an open wound in need of tending, too . . . at least that's how I felt about it.

Sleep came before I had finished my story completely. Josie eventually came down and joined us. She, too, found it fascinating to hear some more of what all I'd been through, even though I had told her most of the story before. I think it was the fact that now she realized how much Noah had been on my mind and in my heart the whole time.

Chapter 30

Day came, and I found myself tucked under Noah's protective arm. I felt calm waking up next to Noah on the basement floor. I watched him sleep for a moment or two, before the phone's ringing woke him up. He smiled and my heart melted.

Everyone was looking for this person or that. Ferrell checked in, letting his mother know he had survived the night.

Noah called and checked in with his superior officer and got his military matters squared away. They were going to send a car for him within the hour.

"They'll drop you off, too," he told me and nodded at Josie. "Your car . . . Well, I think it's gone unless you want to put a lot of money into it."

Josie blew out hot air and shook her head. "It ran really good, too."

"I'll have it towed to the house, Josie, if you want to keep it. If not, we'll just get you another one," I assured her.

"Yeah, because it's not like you're poor," Mrs. Price added.

"And, Mrs. Price, you just don't know how thankful

I am for your hospitality. And I'll be sure to pass on
your concerns to my husband," I said.

"You do that . . . and tell him the next time he wants
to reach out to the black people, he needs to bring his
white self down here . . . don't be sending his girl
Friday," replied Mrs. Price.

I laughed and agreed. I realized then she hadn't
meant anything personal against me the day before.
She was just angry and frustrated, and I felt her pain
completely. I wanted so badly to tell her the truth, but
I couldn't see where it would help anything. No one
would believe her, and she'd be unable to prove it.
Theo had seen to that.

The black military limo pulled up, and we all climbed
in. The driver knew who I was as he had been informed
that I was there when Noah called in. I had a feeling
that Noah was going to be doing nothing but filling out
reports until the cows came home, but he and I had already devised a story as to the reason I was where I was
when I was there. It was a story that was going to save my
behind, because I knew, Theo would be receiving a copy
of the report. There had probably been one sent to him
in Washington the moment the military had been made
aware that I was at Mrs. Price's house.

The driver took Josie and me home first. The gate
security guard looked in the car, with curiosity showing on
his face, as I'm sure he only then realized I wasn't in the
house. Josie went to her quarters, which were in the back.

"Mrs. Fairbanks. I was not aware tha . . . I mean, welcome home," the guard stammered.

"I see you were missed," Noah whispered over his
shoulder. I tapped the back of his neck, shushing him.
He snickered under his breath.

It had been unspoken between us at Mrs. Price's
house, but we both knew, today would not be the last
time we would see each other.

Chapter 31

I was barely in the house before the butler brought me the phone. It was Theo. "Emma! Where have you been?" he screamed.

"I was out with Josie and—"

"You promised me!"

"And I kept that promise. I was out with Josie. We were having ice cream and—"

"Why did you have to have ice cream in Watts, for crying out loud? I swear you bring trouble! It's like you're a magnet!"

"A jinx," I added, speaking under my breath. He heard me and stopped speaking abruptly.

"I didn't say that. You're putting words in my mouth. Listen to me. Can you please just stay at home? Don't shop. Don't go to the movies. Don't even go over to Josie's quarters, okay? Stay away from black people . . . just . . . just stay away."

"Okay, Theo," I agreed. "When will you be home?"

"We've had some delays, for obvious reasons, and so I'll be in conferences for another few weeks."

"Fine." I figured I should give him one more chance to prove that I was worth more to him than what Mrs. Price had said. "Theo, I was thinking that we should start a family."

"We'll talk when I get home. This is not the time to talk about that," he said, using the tone that told me his answer without him even having to speak. No, I would not be having Theo Fairbanks's child any time soon, and I could speculate on the reasons all day long if I wanted to . . . which I didn't.

"Fine."

Josie was watching the news when I knocked on her door and entered before she invited me. "Look at this mess," she said, pointing at the television. Only one station had coverage from the air. The aerial shots of the fires were emotional and evoked many feelings. From the ground, we could only hear the people chanting, "Burn, baby, burn."

Josie's phone rang. I could see that she was too distracted to answer it, so I did.

"Hello, Josie? This is Noah."

"Noah . . ."

"Em'rald, is this you?"

"Yes."

"I was calling Josie to give you a message for me. I wanted you to call me."

"Well, funny . . . isn't it?" I said, trying to control my brain.

"Well, not funny ha-ha so much as funny strange," he said, sounding serious and thought filled.

"Noah . . . I—"

"Can you get away?" he blurted.

"Yes. I won't even be missed."

* * *

When Noah came to pick me up at the gate, I simply got in the car with him. It was just that easy. Perhaps all my public speaking left security with no questions about my coming and going. They had to figure I was on my way to somewhere to speak to the military on my views of the riot. Little did they know, the riot in the streets of Watts was not the first thing on my mind right now . . . although, I figured I would have plenty of time to get back to it.

We drove for over an hour up the coast, to Oxnard. Noah was stationed at the military base there. He'd been living on base for some time now, and so he knew the town well. Parking the military vehicle at the north gate, we exchanged it for his own car and left for a waterfront hotel.

The water was clear and sparkling, and I felt calmer and more relaxed with each passing moment with Noah. I'd done a lot of things in my life, but for some reason being with Noah today felt like the most illicit, the most dangerous thing—yet the most right—at the same time. Nonetheless, Theo was on my mind constantly. I felt as though he was behind me every minute.

As soon as we entered the hotel room, Noah pulled me into his arms. His kiss was as sweet as I remembered, and I wrapped my arms around him as tight as I could, hoping we could kiss forever. His hands wandered down my back to my zipper, where he freed me from the dress I wore.

Onto the bed we tumbled. With the fever we'd shared only once before, we rushed into oneness. Noah was relentless and hungry, and I was beyond that, wrapping my legs around him, urging him deeper and deeper into me. I cried out his name, and he kissed me into silence. Rolling over, I climbed on top of him, kissing his smooth chest and taut belly, and then, urging him to hardness again, I slid down on his want and rode him for what felt like hours.

His fingers ran through my hair; and his large, strong hands, down my body, visiting all the places he remembered and some he'd not had a chance to find on our first encounter.

Rolling over on top of me, he renewed his powerful thrusts, bringing me to song as I called out his name. It was then that the familiar feeling in my belly began to build. I realized then, and only from having read books on the topic, that I was having an orgasm . . . only the second in my life, as Noah had helped me achieve the first one as well.

"You feel it?" he asked me, rocking his body against mine, making sure he hit all the sensitive spots. I began to jerk and spasm while allowing the orgasm to take me over. Gripping the sheet for dear life, I nearly lost my mind when Noah lifted my legs over his shoulders and entered me again. He was on an endless ride, and I was a willing passenger. Finally, bursting forth, he cried out in his ecstasy.

After the moment, we lay in each other's arms, breathing heavily. Breathless, I confessed, "I haven't had sex since the day JFK died."

Noah's eyes widened and then closed again. "You're lyin'."

"My husband is homosexual. He won't touch me. The only reason we did it that day was because his mother had died and we were both grieving. I love him, I do, but it's not the same . . . I don't want to talk about it, Noah," I said, allowing the tears to fall. With his gentle hands, he wiped my tears away.

"I understand," he told me.

Sleep came over us, and I dreamed again about my childhood. It had been a while since I'd had that particular dream, but sleeping with Noah, I wasn't surprised. Noah was looking at me when I woke up. He was smiling.

"I still love you. I always have," he said. I began stroking his manhood, hoping there would be another round of bliss before I had to leave. It was as if he read my mind, and again, we went at each other's sex as if it was to be the last time for both of us . . . not just me.

When Noah brought me home, I appeared as I had when I left. "Thank you, soldier," I said to him through the window of the car as I instructed the security guard to see him off.

I wasn't worried about the cold send-off, as I knew I would be seeing him again tomorrow, and I couldn't wait.

The days were blissful for Noah and me. Walks along Port Hueneme Beach were memorable, and I would keep them in my heart forever. It was nearly a miracle that no one seemed to notice us. It was as if we were a black couple, minding our own business, or maybe times had changed enough, to where interracial relationships were becoming acceptable. I also wore sunglasses and a large, floppy sun hat. Often on the military bases, black soldiers would live with the wives they'd brought back from foreign countries, and maybe that's what people thought when they saw me and Noah together. Whatever the reasons, no one bothered us. Maybe they knew we only had a few more days together. We sure didn't.

We took pictures in a little photo booth. I had taken off my sunglasses and large hat to make sure my face was clearly seen in the pictures. Then I cut one real small to put in the locket.

"Now I'm sure this thing will start bringing me nothing but trouble," Noah said and laughed.

We made love slowly that afternoon, interrupted only by the phone ringing. Only one person knew we were there . . . Ferrell. Noah picked up. His facial expression dropped, and his face twisted. "Shipping out?" Noah asked. "When?"

"Noah, what's happened?" I asked him as soon as he hung up the phone.

"I've got to get back to the base. We're being deployed," he answered solemnly.

"Where? Can you tell me?"

"No, it's classified information. I can't . . . I . . . I have to send you home in a cab. I'll call you as soon as I can."

"Noah, I want to leave my husband. I want you to take me away. We could go to Canada and . . ."

"No, now you know that's not right. That man is your husband, no matter what . . ." He paused. "It's just not right. Hell, this isn't right, but . . ."

"Noah, this is right . . . this is the way it's supposed to be. You and me together . . . please, Noah, let's run away. I'm your wife, please . . ."

"Em'rald, you go through things . . . you don't go around them," he said . . . or was it Mr. Garcia?

"Will you come after me?"

"As soon as I can."

Chapter 32

When I got home, my heart about jumped out of my chest, seeing the limo parked out front. It could only mean one thing: Theo was home early.

I took a deep breath and entered the house as if I'd been on a shopping spree. He was sitting in his swivel chair that faced the large window. He'd no doubt seen *me* get out of the cab that Noah had sent me home in. He turned slowly to me, with his fingertips touching the bridge of his nose. Slowly, he lowered them. His eyes blazed against his otherwise calm expression.

"Where have you been, Emerald?" he asked me. I'd only heard him use my full name on one or two occasions.

"Out," I answered briefly, hoping that would be good enough for him. I turned to leave, but he was up on his feet and gripping my arm tightly, catching me.

"Out where?"

"Theo, I . . ."

"Just a little respect . . . That's all I asked for from you when I found you. I thought to myself, This little, dirty woman can't possibly know how good life would be with a man like me. And then, when I found out the truth . . . that you were just some high yella nigra, I figured, surely, she would never betray me, because I'm the best thing she could ever hope for." Theo then laughed wickedly. "But I see I was wrong. Give you people an inch and you start thinking you own the whole damn road!"

"Theo, you're scaring me. . . ."

"Be afraid, Emerald, be very afraid, feel guilty, have nightmares, because everything bad that could happen to Noah Sampson is your fault."

"What are you talking about?"

"He's on his way to Vietnam. If he makes it back alive, God bless him and America."

Theo slung my arm loose and went back to his chair, swiveling it back around, facing the window.

My mind scattered. I wanted to scream. I wanted to tear his eyes out. How selfish he was. He didn't want me, but he didn't want Noah to have me, either. He was more of a man than I realized . . . jealous and possessive.

I ran out to Josie's quarters.

Chapter 33

It was weeks before Theo and I spoke, civilly or otherwise. He disgusted me, and I was afraid that those words of disdain would leave my lips before anything else. I was glued to the television, watching the news, hoping to get word about the troops landing in Vietnam. Still, the riots and other things clouded that information out, pushing it to the back.

It was on a Friday, late. I knew Theo had retired, but I saw his light on in his room. I had taken to sleeping in another room of the house . . . as far from his as I could get.

I knocked on his door. He answered by inviting me in. I don't know who he was expecting, but he seemed a little surprised it was me. He was in bed, reading. Pulling off his glasses, he looked at me.

"Look what the cat dragged in," he said sarcastically.

"How badly do you want the Senate?" I asked him.

"Pretty bad, I'd say."

"Do you want it with all your heart and soul?"

"Sure. What are you getting at, Em?" he asked, showing his impatience.

"Well, I hope you want it as badly as I want this baby, because I'm not getting rid of it for you or anybody."

He slowly rose and sat on the side of the bed, running his fingers through his thick dark hair. I could hear him blowing out hot air. "Damn you," he mumbled under his breath.

"I have a few suggestions, if you want to hear them."

He looked up at me; his face was strained and showing the growing tension. "What are they?"

"Josie has been seeing a young man from town and is willing to say the baby is hers. But she and the child must be allowed to live in this house with me. I am willing to give up my child to a black woman, the same way my mother gave me up to a white one . . . and for the same reason . . . a better life," I said, tasting the bitterness in my mouth.

"What about your pregnancy? How will you explain it?"

I moved to the door and locked it. Turning back to him, I allowed a wicked grin to cross my lips. "I'm sure you know I've been pregnant before and . . . lost it," I said, choosing my words carefully. "I suppose I'm prone that way." Strolling catlike to the bed, I slid under the silk sheets. "I suggest you tell your lover that you'll be a little tied up the next few weeks. You and your wife have decided to start a family. Good night, husband," I said, turning my back to him.

Chapter 34

Surprisingly enough, over the next few months, Theo and I got along better than we ever had. Perhaps it was the fact that we had an understanding between us now. He knew I loved Noah Sampson—period. My days of being fickle and confused were over. I knew how I felt. I knew who I was, and from that point forward, I always would. Sure, I never heard from Noah again, but just knowing I had his child inside me, even if Noah was dead, convinced me that we would always be together in spirit. I knew if he had died, he had died with my locket around his neck, and if he'd survived, one day he'd come for me . . . if he could.

Josie was only mildly inconvenienced by having to wear a pillow under her clothing, and since she was no longer seeing the young man from town, her being an unwed mother in the 1960s just gave me another platform for public speaking: educating young minority women on the use of the pill and other contraceptives.

Chapter 35

The year 1966 brought the Beach Boys and their good vibrations and a slew of contractions, which alerted me that Scott was soon to make an appearance. The night Scott was born, Theo was out of town, so in the house there was only Josie and me, as I had recently fired the regular staff. Our plan was nearly scientific, except for the fact that babies know nothing about science. The plan was to call my midwife when the time came. She would come deliver my baby, handing it over to Josie, and then would assist me in a staged miscarriage for the media. She'd been paid handsomely to lie about my baby, and it was all set up. When my water broke, I put a call to her to come immediately, but a traffic jam delayed her arrival, and she did not make it on time, and Josie had no choice but to take me to the local hospital, where I delivered Scott.

Theo flew in the next morning. When he entered my hospital room, his expression was blank.

"I'm sorry, Theo. I'm so sorry," I cried, knowing that all my talk was useless now. I'd had my black baby and ruined his career.

"What are you sorry about?" he asked.

"The baby. I haven't seen him yet, but—"

"Well, I have, and, well, Emma, frankly, he's a handsome little lad."

"He is?" I asked, sounding stuffy from crying.

About that time, the nurse came in the room, with Scott bundled up in her arms. Handing him to me, I pulled back the blanket and nearly lost my breath. Surely, Theo had switched my baby. Surely, he had paid someone to do this horrible, unspeakable thing.

"Where's my baby!" I screamed, looking at the chubby pink baby in the blanket. "You bastard! You fuckin' bastard!" I screamed. I wanted nothing more than to tear his eyes out and tried to get out of the bed, without dropping the baby.

Theo asked the nurse to leave.

"I can get the doctor," the nurse said, quickly scooting out of the room.

"You horrible, horrible man . . . where is my baby?" I growled, moaning then like a wounded animal. With all the strength I had left, I was going to kill him, but I knew I first needed to know where my baby was.

"Em, . . . this is your baby. I haven't done anything. I just got here. This is your baby. I swear it." Theo took the baby from my lap, where I had abandoned him, unable to touch him.

"But he's white," I sniveled.

"Yes." Theo grinned. "Yes, he is."

I thought about what my mother had told me about my father and how white his skin was . . . Creole man, she'd called him. No doubt, I carried his dominant genes, and they were even stronger than Noah's.

"My baby?" I asked, my voice now just above a humble peep while I reached out for the newborn. Theo handed him back to me, and once in my arms, I gave him a once-over, looking for any traces of Noah. It was only the broad nose, lips, and spots of melatonin on his back that gave away his ethnicity.

Chapter 36

The *L.A. Times* reported that the Fairbankses took their newborn son home after a little over a week. Their housekeeper, Josie, was reported to have lost her baby at home but was recovering nicely.

It took a while before Noah's features began to show in our son, and even then, it was only in ways I could see. As Scott grew I saw it more and more. The little way he would wrinkle his nose when being told to do something he didn't really want to do, the way he would throw his head back when he laughed—and his smile, his perfectly pure smile.

Perhaps Theo knew that Scott was my only joy, because he never pressured me to be a part of his life in any way, shape, or form, and aside from my supportive public appearances by his side, I never asked to be. I enjoyed my privacy and watching my son grow. I wanted for nothing . . . except Noah's return.

Epilogue

"I would like to say your grandmother will be just fine but . . . ," the doctor said to Thea, who waited anxiously, standing—pacing—in the waiting room.

Scott had been called but had yet to arrive at the emergency room, where Emma had been brought.

"What's wrong with her?" the young-looking Noah asked. He felt the need to know what had caused this old woman to clutch his grandfather's locket, which hung around his neck, and then pass out that way.

He had been watching her. Even though the granddaughter was very pretty and was coming on to him, he had been watching the old lady out of the corner of his eye. While at the festival, where Noah sold antique jewelry, the old white woman had spied the locket, grabbing it up immediately. It was almost as if she had planned to take it, like it was hers—as if she had just found something lost for many years. She'd even gasped a little under her breath.

"Well, it's hard to say. It wasn't a heart attack. It wasn't that," the doctor said, trying to use an assuring tone, one he'd practiced for a long time. He didn't want to worry the girl and her friend, although he was very concerned. He truly didn't know what had caused her heart to go faint the way it had.

"Can I see her?" Thea asked.

"Oh yes, she asked to see you . . . both of you," the doctor said.

Thea looked at the young man, who shrugged. He had come to the hospital. He'd felt the need. After all, the woman had had some kind of reaction to his table. He felt sort of responsible. Thea wanted to hold him a little responsible, too, but that was just her personality.

"Don't you need to get back to the festival to tend to your table?" Thea asked, not meaning to sound rude.

"My buddy is at my table. I'm not worried about it," he said, not catching her tone. "Besides, I want to see your grandmother. I want to make sure she's okay."

Thea hesitated and then, following the doctor, allowed the young man to join her in what Thea would have rather had been a private moment with her grandmother.

When they both entered the room, Emma's focus went immediately to the young man, and although Thea spoke to her, Emma did not take her eyes off him.

"You're Noah Sampson, aren't you?" Emma finally asked him, cutting Thea off mid-ramble. Thea looked at the young man now as he approached the bed. He was intrigued by this strange woman's aura and curious as to how she knew his full name. He had never done this festival before; he had never seen her before. He'd only been out here going to college for the last two years, and before that, he'd lived in Shreveport, Louisiana, where he was born and raised. There was no way this white woman, this apparently well-off white woman, knew him.

"Yes, yes, I am," Noah said. Emma's eyes closed tightly, and again, she clutched the locket to her chest.

"Grandma, what is that you're holding?" Thea asked now, holding her palms out to receive the small trinket from Emma, who only now showed the treasure openly.

"I'm holding my life." Emma smiled weakly as a tear ran down her face into her ear. "I've been waiting for it for years . . . and it's finally here."

Thea was caught totally off guard by her grandmother's words and emotions. She was embarrassed for her and unconsciously moved herself between the bed and Noah, blocking him from getting any closer. It was obvious to Thea that his presence was upsetting her.

"Could you excuse us?" Thea said to Noah over her shoulder. He stepped back, embarrassed a little at the thought that he possibly had something to do with making the woman cry.

"I'm sorry, I . . ," he stumbled.

Just then, Scott burst into the room. His face was tense with concern. "Mother, are you all right?"

Emma smiled and nodded. "Scott, this is your father, Noah Sampson," she said, introducing the young man to her son as if Scott would have any reason to know who this young man was—or believe that he could possibly be his father. Scott nodded at him and quickly put his attention back on his mother. It was obvious she was delusional.

"Mother, how are you feeling?" Scott asked her.

"Noah came back to me. He said he would," she said, showing Scott the locket. He took the piece of jewelry from his mother's hand, and opening it, he saw inside a picture of Emma as a young woman of twenty-five or so. "Although he was awfully late," she added. "And you know what I say about late folks."

Turning to the young Noah, she asked, "So, Noah, what took you so damn long?"

Noah had seen the picture inside the locket before; however, he had never known who the woman was until today . . . Well, he had never believed the woman existed until this very moment.

Noah stepped closer to the bed now, getting a closer look at the woman whose looks had, surely, been perfection at one time, and whose dancing green eyes still held a spark, which had once been, no doubt, a blazing fire and a spellbinding power. His grandfather had spoken of the green-eyed black woman with white skin often enough . . . often enough to cause him to dream about her.

"You're Em'rald," Noah said. "Em'rald Jackson."

Emma smiled and softly touched Noah's face. "And you're my husband." She grinned, and then, glancing at the locket once more, she looked at him again. "And I'm ready to go now," she said, slowly closing her eyes.

When her eyes opened, Noah, reaching out his hand, took the locket from her and slipped it around her neck, allowing it to hang from the gold chain. He pulled her into his embrace and kissed her tenderly. "I told you I would come back for you," he said. "You jinx, you."

"Yeah, but what took you so damn long?" Emerald asked, sounding sassy as always. "I spent my whole life wasting away . . . doing nothing but waiting for you," she fussed. "You don't know what I've been dealing with while you've been gone . . . raising that boy by myself."

Noah smiled and then wrapped his arm around her shoulder as she gripped him tightly around his waist as they strolled together, bare foot, along the cool sands of Port Hueneme Beach, their backs heated by the summer sun. "Tell me all about it, Em'rald. We've got all the time in the world."

* * *

Scott Fairbanks leaned back in his chair, folding his arms across his chest, satisfied with the words on the screen of his laptop. He had finished his first novel, entitled *Emerald*. It was the story of his mother, Emerald Jackson, and whether true or a fantasy, whether she was just another white woman with a vivid imagination or truly a black woman who had spent her life under the weight of a promise, she was one hell of a woman and worth every moment of her memory.

"Dad," he heard Thea call. "The limos are here." Her voice was heavy with contained grief. Thea had been strong for him, but he knew one day that she would have to find release from her pain, as he had in penning the novel he had just completed.

Knowing his mother had been full of so much life and color made his memories better. Knowing that his father was Noah Sampson, a black man, and that he had half brothers now to meet and get to know, made his life more interesting. What a newfound perspective he had on life now, knowing that everything was not as it had seemed growing up, as he had always taken his father's coldness personally, as if he was at fault—but it wasn't that way at all. Scott realized now that his life was by arrangement, an arrangement made between his mother and a man torn between his true feelings for her and his sexual persuasion. How certain Theo Fairbanks had been of his orientation, as he had been sure about everything he did . . . that is, until a colored woman and a summer day changed his life and way of thinking.

Looking at his watch, Scott realized it was, indeed, time to head out to Queen of the Heavens Cemetery. His mother had always hated when he was late. She would always say, "If you not gonna come when expected, don't bother coming at all." And now he understood what she meant.